Colin Andrew Brown

The Heart Explosion

Published by Heart Voyance Enterprises Ltd

Cover design: Chloe Brown

Published by Heart Voyance Enterprises Ltd

www.heartvoyance.co.uk

ISBN: 978-0-9570515-1-5

Our whole business therefore in this life is to restore to health the eye of the heart whereby God may be seen.

St. Augustine (354-430)

Dedicated to:
Margaret Jones,
Petra Brown
and Heart People throughout the World.

Acknowledgements

I would like to thank the following for their comments and enthusiasm in reviewing this book: Petra, Chloe, Leah, Ann Lechareas, Denise Graf, Fiona Schenk, Karin Danner, Monika Bernegg, Olga Rutman, Patricia Latorre, Robert Walls, Uli Burger, Verena Deeken, Tanis Helliwell, Karin Wagner and all at Kleinerschreibwerkstatt. Special thanks to Jerry Gardner for his fine eye and endless motivation.

I would like to thank my family for giving me the time and space to write, and to Chloe for creating the cover.

For technical advice I would like to thank Peter McHugh and Alexander Rutman.

For confirmation of the Future of Heart Intuition I would like to thank Rollin McCraty from HeartMath Institute.

Heart-thinking review and advice came from Daniel Dominguez and Mark Riccio. The whole subject would not be here if it were not for the dedicated work of Florin Lowndes.

Table of Contents

1

A Trip to London

It was a Saturday morning when Cameron Trevelyn awoke from his dream world to brilliant sunshine, a nagging intuition pulling at his heart. He could hear the crows outside as they gathered in the nearby trees for their morning chorus. The vivid smells of spring growth, fuelled by the overnight rain, poured through the open window. For the first time in what seemed like forever, he felt alive.

So what was nagging at him? Cameron switched his attention back to his heart. He felt the familiar glowing expansion, a sign that his intuition was trying to tell him something. He understood the message, half in a picture and half in an almost spoken voice. "Make a trip to London." The message had a feeling of urgency with it, telling him to go immediately. This was going to be fun.

He called out his instructions to the House Com, asking it to find him the best way to get to London. He walked to the nearest screen on the wall of the bedroom. A suggested itinerary was already listed for the journey, May 7th, 2050, Castleton to London– Euston printed at the top, followed by details of a two hour journey into the capital. If he took an E-car to Macclesfield train station he would arrive at Euston before one o'clock.

He got dressed and checked himself in the mirror. His blond hair camouflaged the early grey hairs. Despite the mourning of the past two years, life had left his face appearing young, even if he was approaching forty. Replacing his cycling by walking had ensured that he had kept his tall figure trim. He had no idea if his clothes were fashionable or not, this had not interested him in a long time.

It was a single seat three wheeler E-car that arrived and he let it drive him to the station, not bothering to switch over to manual. The car arrived on time and he strolled over to the platform. There were about fifteen people waiting for the train. A small family was at the loading bay, watching their luggage box being shifted from their hire car by the robot crane, to be left ready on the end of the platform for transfer onto the train. He shut his eyes and looked up into the sun, a smile on his face. He had only a few minutes to wait before the train arrived and he got on.

After settling into a corner seat, he read in peace for a while. His mind turned to his dream last night. Some scenes he could remember, others were vague. The part of the dream which was strangest and perhaps most wonderful he could only half recall, something about a brilliant white light emanating from a strangely shaped crystal. The weight of mourning, like a black stone in his heart, had suddenly disappeared and his intuitive capabilities were back to full strength. Was this change also connected to this dream?

His pondering stopped when the train passed the city boundaries. He had forgotten the confusing atmosphere in the larger towns; it was like walking through a grey foggy soup, except this soup was not edible. The atmosphere had a certain electric charge to it, which he did not remember from his last visit. Was the city society losing itself further in this self-generated chaos?

*

Professor Beck sat at his desk in his university office. He had a small office, just six meters by four. Two sides of the office contained wall-to-wall books, mostly about physics. He had an old-fashioned wooden desk with built-in drawers, something made in the first half of the twentieth century. His only technical device was an old fashioned terminal of monitor, keyboard and mouse, something which his colleagues found almost as amusing as his need for paper printouts.

He was going through a pile of them now on his desk, catching up with his extra-curricula tasks on this glorious Saturday morning. He had gone through various patent applications, seeing nothing worthy of note before he came upon this paper. It had the clear hand of a scientist, the terminology being correct, the phrasing being so familiar as to be a joy to read. It was a pity the contents were pure nonsense.

It was a long forgotten dream to invent the perfect energy machine, a dinosaur idea from the nineteenth century scientists. They had tried so often to create such a machine, before finally realizing it was impossible. How could it be that in this day and age this idea could still be alive, he thought?

Yet here was a description of exactly such a machine. In exact detail it explained what the construction was, how it was going to work. He was impressed with the high standard of the patent application but found the basic idea of what it was meant to do just nonsense. He could not accept it.

Professor Beck had taken on this contract to earn some additional money. It was quite simple. He would be sent patent applications and he had to go through them and check for any scientific and engineering advancements, no matter how far-fetched. Anything worthy of note he was to pass back to the client with his added comments. There were many new patents nowadays; great innovations were coming through which were having a noticeable effect on everyday life, so this was an additional money-earner that he had accepted with joy. As with this one, many of the patent applications he was being asked to review came from the governing body of the Heart Voyance Schools. In fact over the months he had noticed that most of the interesting patents came from that source and the rest were quite boring in comparison. This had awakened his curiosity about the schools, and he thought that perhaps he would take a more detailed look at them. But somehow he had never got round to it.

What to do in this case though? It was fine to add his opinions to interesting patents and pass them on. He hoped his masters made good use of the expert advice they were getting. Strangely enough he had had little feedback from them, given the expense of the contract. So, should he send this patent back with his comments, or should he just ignore it, for the pseudo-science it was?

Professor Beck made his decision. Perhaps it was the fact that the patent was clearly written by a scientist that moved him to recognize it. He added his comments to the patent and sent it off to his employer.

Little did he realize that he had set off a chain of catastrophic happenings, which challenged the very survival of the Heart Voyance Schools in which he was so interested in. He simply continued with his work, unaffected by the course of events he had set in motion.

*

Arriving at Euston, Cameron smiled inwardly, enjoying the aspect of having no idea what he was going to be doing. He had lived intuitively before but in the years of mourning he had functioned more like a robot. It felt comfortable to be led through the city, without knowing the destination. He headed straight for the map of the Underground and his eyes soon focused on Pimlico tube station. Was he to head there? He checked by looking away, focusing on another station and seeing if that had the same impulse behind it. It didn't. So Pimlico was where he would go.

Before setting off, he turned around, his back to the wall, and looked at everyone passing by. The scene here had barely changed in decades. Hundreds of people were busy going their way. Some were lost in the electronic media they carried, be it films displayed on the inside of spectacles (only in one eye when they were walking around) or, if you looked carefully, you could see the small earpieces of their audio device. They were moving fast, intent on their destination, or the play of events going through their minds. Perhaps one in twenty was aware of their surroundings and fewer people than that were smiling. Whatever world they were in, they carried a dirty cloud of emotions around with them. He always felt sad when watching them and wished that it could be different.

He set off again, straight down the Victoria line. Getting off at the station, his eye was caught by posters on the wall advertising a new William Blake exhibition at the Tate Gallery. Pleased with himself that he still seemed to be on track, he set off, wondering what he would find at the gallery.

*

Elaine Gordon awoke, knowing this would be the day. Had she managed it, to use her mind to send a request to meet a person she had never seen before? She had pictured in her mind the two of them meeting today and had asked him to agree. She had felt the acknowledgement but was unsure whether to believe it. All the books she had secretly read had said such a thing was possible, but actually doing it felt scary. Well, she would know before evening whether it had worked. Her Mum would have taken her to the nearest psychiatrist if Elaine were stupid enough to tell her what she was doing. She had learnt long ago it was pointless to talk to her Mum about such things.

She got up and checked her alarm clock. The House Com should have noticed her awakening and switched off the clock, but it had been unreliable recently. Elaine looked around her room. Most of the walls were covered with pictures of rock stars and actors just like any other teenager's. However, one corner was dedicated to articles and pictures of the Heart Voyance Schools around the world. Central was the first article she had seen about Cameron Trevelyn, on his work with the police as a Truthsayer, printed in a magazine about three years ago. It was this article which first brought her attention to the Heart Voyance Schools and in particular the one in Castleton where Cameron worked. It was her dream to attend a Heart Voyance School.

Elaine went downstairs and started making herself some breakfast as she heard her brother trotting down the stairs, two at a time. He stamped into the kitchen. "So, today you finally get us to go see your crazy artist exhibition," he said, a half smile creeping its way across his face. "It's lucky it's the Tate Gallery, you wouldn't find me dead in some dive in Clapham. Art's just a waste of time anyway, bleedin' hearts who can't find a decent way to live. Just like you to be interested in a scatological impressionist like Blake. I get better pictures than his on my I-view and in 3D too. He died hungry in poverty just like you will, loser."

Elaine fought her automatic impulse to argue back, holding her mouth shut, willing herself to silence. She knew Sam was just trying to get her angry so their parents would have an excuse to call the outing off.

Her parents appeared for breakfast, Janine not going beyond her customary boiled egg and black coffee, Jack having his regular weekend breakfast of a bacon sandwich in brown toasted bread. Janine gave Elaine a big smile, "I'm so glad we are all going to see your artist. I'm sure after this you can concentrate on your school work and not on that silly nonsense of yours."

"Brain the size of a pea, we're fortunate she can read and write," said Jack. "Pictures are more fitting for our little thickie daughter, she would be as much use at university as a slug in a lettuce field."

"Ssh," added Janine, half-heartedly.

Elaine had to clench her jaws together to hold her emotions back. One way or another, she would be gone from here very soon. She thought about her best friend Mole. It seemed odd to other people that she used a nickname for her own grandfather. He asked her to use the name and it was ages later that she found out that with this name he had a hidden life beyond public view, where he was also successful.

Elaine was still amazed that such an incredible man as Mole could have produced such a conservative daughter as Janine. Away from Mole's public face he was versatile, always looking at everything from a new angle. Janine was just suffocating. Elaine could not stand this claustrophobic family atmosphere. She wanted fresh air and she was going to get it.

*

The exhibition rooms were dark. William Blake's paintings were often very small, so people gathered close to them. In one corner of a room, Cameron came across some of Blake's early pencil sketches of sculptures in Westminster Abbey. He was fascinated by how well drawn they were - it showed that Blake was very accurate in what he was depicting. Blake's visionary paintings were different. The figures looked odd and often seemed to show a reflection of Blake's own appearance. Blake could draw well, so when he was drawing his visions, the original image itself must have had an aspect of his own appearance in them. It was as if he were seeing the visions through a filter of his own mind, which lent the appearances strange hues, colors and contours. This confirmed to Cameron something he had always guessed at - that when mystics had visions, they often had an aspect of their own appearance in the work they created.

He was glad to have had a chance to make this observation about mystical paintings. His focus widened to take in more of the viewing public. He wondered if he had come here just to better understand esoteric art. Standing still for a moment and focusing in on himself, he suddenly realized this was not the case. He was here to meet someone. Intrigued, he continued wandering around, enjoying the paintings. He wondered what Blake would think about the current situation, with so many people walking about in his beloved London, half asleep, not wishing to wake up.

He came across one picture, one of the few large paintings in the exhibition, "An Allegory of the Spiritual Condition of Man". The title alone amused him, but the picture itself he found absorbing, with its various figures arranged around the canvas in a clear structure. He appreciated this style of art. He stopped and stared at the picture, mesmerized by it.

After a while he became aware of someone standing next to him. He looked to one side and noticed a teenage girl standing there. She was about fifteen years old, below average height, quite thin, brown tussled hair around an oval face with bright inquisitive eyes. She was absorbed in the painting and paid him no attention. His heart told him straight away that this was the person he had come to see. He was rather surprised, as he had half expected someone mature. He looked at her considerately and opened up his intuition. He began to pick up information about her. She was going to a state school but did not fit in, she had a big heart but only a few friends. She had trouble at home, her parents and brother were Sleepers. She was different, fully human, almost from a different planet. Born into a family of Sleepers, that must be very hard. Just to survive and keep herself intact would have been difficult. It was clear why they were meeting: she wanted to go to his school. He was left with a vague feeling she was important, but he had no idea why.

For a moment just the two of them were left looking at the picture. Cameron decided he would open the conversation, "This painting, I just love the mixture of structure and art, one can contemplate it for ages. It's fascinating, isn't it?"

She turned towards him. Her face looked slightly shocked as she obviously recognized him, then she began a nervous smile. "It's just odd really," replied the girl, "the way the figures are just hanging in mid air. Then you see it's got form, it flows up and down and the women look like angels. So you follow the figures up and down in their pattern. It leaves you so calm."

Elaine could not hold herself back any longer. "You're Cameron Trevelyn aren't you?" she said.

"Sometimes," he replied. He gave a small grin to let her know he was joking.

Her face lit up, "I've wanted to meet you for ages. I want to go to your school."

He nodded in reply. She tilted her head to one side as realization took her and then said, "You already knew I wanted to go to your school, didn't you?"

Cameron looked at her and thought things through quickly. She was a bit old to start at the school, as they generally preferred someone younger. But his colleagues would trust him on this one, especially when they learnt how open she was. Her parents were such straight types that it would take some effort to win them over to the idea of their daughter going to a Heart Voyance School. They would not pay for it either. She was going to be another one for the school's scholarship fund.

She was special though. She would make a great addition to the school. There was something else about her too. He dwelt on this further. She was not only an ideal candidate for the school; he felt a warm connection to her, as if she had some significance for him as well.

"What's your name?" he asked.

"Elaine Gordon," she replied.

"And you want to attend our school? You know our school is for boarders and you would have to live away from your family and friends."

She nodded, looking intensely at him as she waited for his confirmation.

Cameron thought before answering. His intuition was stronger than before, more consistent and easier to understand. This enhanced ability was going to be a potent addition to his life. He wondered where it would lead him. He also wondered how he was going to convince Elaine's parents to let her go to a strange boarding school.

"Well, Elaine Gordon, I think it's time to meet your parents. I have something to say to them and this might take a while. So it's best to start now."

2

A History Lesson

Elaine was ready. She had tried on her fourth pair of jeans and jumper, finally settling on her favorite purple top. She left the small house that was her new home, shouting a short goodbye. Ginny, a fellow house mate came running down the stairs to give her a quick hug for good luck before she went off to her first day at school.

The walk to school was a short one. The school owned or rented several houses nearby and some of the older pupils lived in them alone. A family lived next door to the house to which she was assigned, and was always available in emergencies. The five girls in the house were aged between thirteen and eighteen, and were good at looking after both themselves and the house.

She stood at the doorway to her new classroom and gazed at that colorful collection, thinking she had walked into a Technicolor zoo, rather than into a light purple, pastel colored classroom. Later she learnt the history of this display. Plume started it off. She always dressed in a coat of bird's feathers, small ones at the back and around the midriff, larger ones around the shoulders. She had originally bought the coat in a flea market. So many feathers fell off it when she moved around she left a trail behind her. You always knew which chair she had sat on by the collection of feathers left behind. She gained the nickname Plumage, quickly shortened to Plume. Later on Elaine found out she spent half an hour every weekend sewing on new feathers. Her acquaintances got used to passing on feathers to her whenever they found them.

Typical of the school, as soon as one person started a trend, half the class joined in. So when Elaine walked in they were in the middle of their animal phase, something that lasted for about three months. Johannes was dressed in brown, trying to look like a bear. Malika, never one to let anyone outdo her, was always dressed in white, usually with feathers and a made-up face which left you in no doubt that she was a swan. Worst was Wheel, who had a whole range of fox-fur clothes, including fox-fur shorts. These were homemade and despite many interrogations, he never revealed where the fur came from. His friend

Jason wanted to be called Mothman when he wore a long coat with moth's wings painted at the back. Unfortunately for him, most people just called him Bugboy and the name stuck long after the coat was gathering dust and neglect.

Something else was also apparent: the class was very quiet compared to her old school.

One of the girls in the classroom saw her, smiled and made her way across to her, stretching out her hand for a handshake. "Hi, I'm Denise, you must be Elaine. Welcome to our class." Denise put her hand on Elaine's shoulder and used it to guide her into the classroom. Elaine was soon surrounded, everyone in the class politely introducing themselves.

In strode a slightly plump woman with blond hair, mid-fifties, Elaine guessed. As the woman reached the front table she turned around and gave a firm, "Good morning", her long skirt swishing about her legs. She looked across at Elaine, her round face smiled and in a quiet voice said, "Hi, I'm Cathy Wittgenstein." She then raised her voice and filled the whole room with her authority. "As you have seen, we welcome a new member to our community. Elaine has grown up in London and knows little of our ways, so I thought the best way of introducing her would be to have a circle lesson. The topic is, the history of our schooling system."

Any concerns Elaine might have had about the class not liking doing a history lesson just for her were immediately put at rest by a few cries of "Yo!" and "Whoopie!" which greeted this announcement. The idea of what a circle lesson entailed also became apparent when everyone busied themselves moving the tables to one side and arranging the chairs in a circle.

Once everyone was settled, one of the other pupils, Jason, started to talk, "Well, it ain't no system, it's a community. It was formed at the beginning of the 2020's, this being the first school, then others followed. So far we have fifty schools across the world, here in the U.K., America, Canada, South Africa and New Zealand, so you could say we are pretty international."

"We can consider ourselves truly international when we have moved into the non-Anglo-Saxon countries," added Cathy.

"Definitely could be. Anyway, we weren't the only schooling system to spring up at this time, there were many alternative systems. Some, like the great Wiccans, were based on previous ideas. Others like us started on new stuff."

"But why did this start off in Castleton?" asked Elaine.

"To be close to the Peak cavern, the big cave in the cleft of the hill. It's dead special," answered Johannes.

Elaine looked puzzled. Seeing her face, the teacher said, "I'll arrange for someone to take you there."

"Not much to say, so, we learn here head and heart. That's it!' said Wheel. He looked up at a corner of the room, taking on an air of being bored. The effect he created was augmented by his fox fur waistcoat, which matched the color of his shoulder length, red-brown straight hair.

"Well, how do you develop someone's Intuition?" asked Elaine.

"The first thing is to find out what sort of Intuition yer good at," replied Jason. Elaine's face crinkled up. "It's like this," he continued. "Wheel here is a crack with animals. He can tell you exactly what is wrong with yer dog long before the vet gets there. I'm a geomancer. Give me a landscape, I'll tell you where to build yer house 'n' stuff. I'm great with metals as well, can really say how to get things well made. So, I mean, metal and stone, that's my thing. Ginny who you live with, is a genius with plants, everything grows when she touches it. Last but by no means least is Malika, here, who can tell you exactly who did what in yer house 'n' exactly why two people are incompatible."

"So you see," added Cathy, "we teach Intuition in four ways. The first is everything to do with stone and landscape. The second is the plant world. The third is animals. Lastly, and quite popular, is people and buildings."

"How do computers fit in?" asked Elaine.

"Computers? We don't do computers. In fact, we have very few computers in the school," answered the teacher.

Malika peered over at Elaine, "But you have a special connection to Coms, don't you? You can do something exceptional with them."

Elaine beamed across the circle to Malika, brushing back her hair from her face. "My friend Mole got me into Coms. I know things with them. I'm not sure how to describe it. But I bet I could be as good with Coms as you are with humans."

"I don't think you need to describe it to us," replied Malika. "But there's no one here who is good with Coms. You're the first. And that makes you unique. And pretty special."

"I'm looking forward to seeing what you can do," said Cathy. "One day you will be teaching us about Intuition with machines."

Elaine looked up and around the circle. A few were nodding their heads at her in acknowledgement. She realized she had found her place. It was weird, she had only been in the room a short while and she felt more genuine acceptance and respect here than ever before. This was working so well. She hoped the other teachers were equally as good.

Cathy stepped in again. "You should also know something about funding. The school charges fees for each child. We also have a fund, which we use when parents cannot or won't pay for the education. This fund was created by ex-pupils and from the university college we have in the Dales. There they patent ideas, which the rest of the world can use. The most helpful ideas are given away free, of course."

Elaine looked skeptical. "Do all the ex-pupils fund the school like that? Why are you telling me about school finances?"

"We have a different attitude towards money and finance', said Wheel. "We learn a lot here about energy and money as being just one form of energy. My parents went to school here and they love providing money for it. It is not a burden for them but a joy. Many of their class do the same. Others have moved and their children go on to different types of school, so they support them instead. It's quite normal to talk about it."

"What's the difference between this and the other mystery schools?" asked Elaine.

"We see ourselves as a bridge between the old world and the new. This is an environment where people live in their hearts, and at the same time maintain their intellect. So we function in head and heart, allowing people to develop their intuition and their empathy at the same time as keeping their intelligence. Many of the other schools are so deeply heart-based that newcomers like yourself, have a great deal of difficulty adjusting to that way of life and understanding how the people function there."

Elaine nodded, then asked, "So how many new people do you get?"

"Not enough," said Cathy.

"You're the first Sleeper I have had the chance to meet," said Jason.

Elaine raised her eyebrows. "Sleeper?"

"That's what we call city people, the people you grew up with," said Jason. "They function in life like they're half-asleep. Too busy functioning within their tightly held society rules, passing each other by as if the other person did not exist. If someone walks past us in the street, we can tell what sort of a mood they are in. It's very difficult to lie to us. We know whether the spoken words match what the person thinks behind the words. That's how the Truthsayers work. We are all a bit of an open book to each other and with empathy and understanding, we put effort in trying to work well together."

"You don't need to tell her," said Malika. "Elaine might have grown up in the city, but she's no Sleeper. She's one of us. One of the Heart People."

Everyone looked at Malika, taking in what she had said and then looking back again at Elaine. Wheel spoke first, "How on earth did you manage to survive in that hostile atmosphere? It must have been very lonely."

Elaine opened her mouth to speak but her throat betrayed her. No words came out. Never before had she met a group of people who had so quickly understood her, not even in her own family. She felt like she had come home.

"You might find that things work more leisurely here. We are not driven by our emotions, even us teenagers," said Malika. "We don't jump into relationships, we take our time. And life is slower, except when it's faster, and then it's really fast, if you get what I mean. You'll like it here."

Elaine certainly hoped so.

3

The Heart Voyance School

Cameron walked across the schoolyard towards the administration house, conscious of the familiar surroundings. The school buildings formed a square, leaving a courtyard in the centre. Like all the buildings in Castleton, they were made out of grey stone, with small windows in white frames. Some of the outside of the buildings looked like two or three town houses joined together, but when you walked through one of the doors, you entered one large room. In this way the school blended in with the rest of the town but still had the spacious rooms it needed. Looking from inside the courtyard, the buildings all looked very contemporary, the windows were much larger, some walls consisting of a single pane of glass. Each "house' was a different shape and size but designed in such a way that together they all still managed to blend into each other to give a harmonious whole.

Cameron stopped in the middle of the courtyard. He was tired and felt his mind slipping into a kind of tunnel vision. In a few minutes he would correct that.

He focused on a random corner of one of the buildings, at a point on a wooden beam where the ground floor met the first floor. He concentrated his focus on the edge of that wooden beam, then opened up his peripheral vision, so he became more aware of what was there on either side of the point he was staring at. He was now aware of about 60 degrees of what was in front of him. At this point, while remaining focused on the edge of the beam and what he could see in his peripheral vision, he took in the sounds and the smells around him. He could hear children talking nearby, and could feel the wind on his face, bringing a feeling of dampness with it. He went back to his visual awareness, and expanded it to a full 180 degrees, taking in all that was in front of him. Then he swung his awareness round in a full 360 degree arc, focusing on everything that was around him. He could not see what was behind him, but he could become aware of it, listening for what was going on, remembering what was there and seeing if he could detect it in any way. Once he had done that, he expanded his awareness further, taking in the sky, air and clouds above him and the solid feeling of the earth beneath his feet.

Finished, now feeling more awake and focused, he turned and faced the administration building. Two of the smaller children had been looking at him the whole time and whispered and giggled at him. Centus, one of the upper school pupils, walked towards him, "I watched you. Your body became more upright, standing straight and obviously more alert. You know, we're taught that in class but it's the first time I have ever seen an adult do it. That was really something!"

"Thank you," said Cameron, a warm smile decorating his face. He walked on.

The administration office was a small building in a corner of the school grounds, with a beautiful garden at the front and a large arbor of rose plants on the approach path. In summer, it looked like you had to go through a tunnel of red roses to reach the entrance door.

Inside the two admin assistants were working away. Cameron smiled as he walked past them and went into his office. He had just enough time to prepare for his next meeting: with Elaine's teachers. He found it odd that they had requested a meeting with him, and began looking back over the past three months that Elaine had been at the school. He guessed it must have been a rough ride.

He was still pondering over Elaine, trying to get a picture of where she was, when the first of the teachers walked in. Daniel Price was grey haired and lean, a calming melancholy personality. He was much loved, having been at the school for over twenty years. Joel Spencer and Cathy Wittgenstein arrived together, deep in conversation from their previous meeting.

At the last minute a fourth person joined them, a woman to whom he could not put a name. She looked like she was in her early thirties, of medium build, with straight, thick black hair ending just below her shoulders. She had large dark eyes, which gave a short smile when she realized he was watching her.

"Hi Cameron, I'm Melody Graves. Perhaps you remember, I went to the Teachers College in the Dales for a ground level diploma. We will be working together on the framework of the new 21-plus further education seminars." Cameron vaguely remembered her being sponsored to go to the college, a hurt woman needing to distance herself from her domineering Sleeper husband. The memory was stuck back somewhere at the beginning of his dark years. His impression of her now was completely different. Here was a confident, attractive woman in the prime of her years, who radiated warmth. He could not keep his eyes off her.

"Cameron, let's start, shall we?" Cathy waded in. "Elaine Gordon. She has been at the school now for three months. Her academic work is very impressive. She is the top of the class as far as mathematics is concerned; she has an amazing ability with numbers, not just able to do advanced mental arithmetic but also to recall huge numbers, way beyond what we would expect, even in a school like this. Her artistic talent is undeveloped but she shows some great potential.

"It's on the social side that we are concerned. Elaine started off withdrawn and seemed to be watching, as if she was waiting for something. We're concerned that she is not fitting in as fast as we hoped for her."

"She's a waste of time and we should get rid of her," said Joel.

There was an uncomfortable pause, as the others turned towards Joel in shocked silence, trying to read why the teacher was being so unexpectedly aggressive. Cameron looked past Joel, trying to take him in without a long eye contact that would strain them both. He couldn't pick up much but he understood enough to realize Joel was walking into a self-created crisis.

'What brought on the change?" asked Cameron, looking back at Cathy.

"Oh, I dunno, I think there is nothing fantastically wrong," Cathy replied, "She's just a teenager from the city, meeting a group of people from a different society and basically messing it up a bit. She was fine for the first few weeks, she got on well with the other pupils with no signs of friction, which we found unusual for that age. She asked the others what abilities they had, could they see auras and elementals, all the usual stuff from a newcomer. Elaine did not rub anyone's back up but she didn't get many answers either. Particularly as she asked all the wrong pupils."

Cameron smiled out of the side of his mouth, "So she hasn't met many people who can see. But we knew this anyway. What do you want to do, throw her out?"

"At last you're talking sense. We waste too much good education on stupid people," threw in Joel.

Cathy's forehead creased in a frown while looking at Joel, before turning back. "Cameron, you found her originally. We wanted to talk with you about what to do with her."

Melody looked puzzled. "Can someone fill me in on how Elaine came to be here?"

Cameron gave a brief overview of his trip to London to meet Elaine, and his long talk with her parents before they gave their permission for her to attend the school.

Melody raised her eyebrows in astonishment. "You went all the way to London and in the middle of the city managed to home in on one picture to meet a girl for the school? How on earth did you manage to keep going in a Dome?"

Joel grinned back at her, "Crazy Cameron can do better than that. Ask him the one about literally finding the skeleton in the cupboard. Who knows what leads him to do these things? A regular little Sherlock Holmes is our Cameron. He can keep going in the murkiest of places," he said, his tone an odd mixture of awe and skepticism.

"OK Joel, this time you're way off," said Cameron. "Elaine wanted to come to the school and it was clear that I was directed to meet her. Following the intuition showed itself correct by the outcome. My instinct remains that she is a very special person, in herself, and that she has some sort of a connection to me. Her academic work shows hints of her qualities - how often do we find someone with such artistic ability that is also highly numeric?

"Has anyone looked into her karmic background? Has she got any previous difficult experiences with heart-intuition that are creating her stress in this life?"

Daniel spoke in his quiet, assured way, "We gave up looking at karmic backgrounds of new pupils a while back, Cameron. We always double-checked with two people doing the research but we never found anything in the background that would give the students problems. Far from it. The whole thing took a great deal of effort. It made little difference, so we decided to discontinue it."

Melody now joined in. "May I suggest, the way forward is simple - we would do best to talk to the poor girl and find out what is troubling her. If she comes from a family of Sleepers, has anyone tried talking to her about how to live in our world?" Melody looked at the faces around the table and it was quite clear that they had not thought of that. She continued, "The important thing is that whoever talks to her must be someone she has trust in. Who is her mentor teacher?"

"I am," said Joel, to an uncomfortable silence.

Unperturbed, Melody had another try, "Cameron, you're the one she managed to get in touch with to be here - she has a strong connection to you. Why don't you meet with her?"

"That appeals, but it's been a couple years since I have had direct dealings with the students. I might easily trip up and say the wrong thing," said Cameron.

"How about if I sat in with you, so it was three of us?" suggested Melody. "I'm used to talking to Sleepers. I can act for the teaching staff, without disturbing the connection between the two of you."

Cameron looked at Melody. Her face was open to him, something he found invigorating. The idea of joining with her in the mentor activities was appealing. He looked at the others carefully. Joel was looking almost positive. Daniel, as usual, had said little, but if he objected he would have spoken. Cathy had a questioning look on her face. Cameron spoke back to her.

"I could get through to her. We won't know if we don't try, and perhaps it's time for me to have contact with the students again. Let's try it Melody's way."

"Well, if that's decided, you don't need me anymore," said Joel, rising from the table. "Melody, if you can inform Elaine that you and Cameron have taken on mentor duties for her, then I am done here." With a small smile of relief, he left the room.

"Can I ask for some help here?" said Melody. "Somehow I just did not understand what was wrong with Elaine."

"Nothing," said Daniel. "At least, if I take you literally, there is nothing wrong with Elaine."

"Let me guess," said Cameron. "Coming into this new environment, she has performed academically quite well but socially has difficulties. She has received no support from her designated mentor, who would be the one to steer her through whatever minor obstacles she would face. You can always have misunderstandings when someone is new to the community and haven't learnt our ways yet." He leaned back in his chair before continuing. "But we now have a pupil thinking about leaving and a mentor who has washed his hands of her. So where is the root of the problem, with Elaine or with Joel?"

"We asked Joel as he was the most intellectual person available, someone who would understand a Sleeper better," said Daniel. "Instead it seems to have set off a crisis in Joel."

"What crisis?" asked Melody.

"Joel has been touched by too much intellectual strain," said Cameron. "It has brought him back to the conflict between intellect and intuition." He leaned forward across the table towards the others. "He is in a difficult situation. Look after him, he adds a great deal to our community. Sooner or later there will come a time of crisis when his input can really make a difference. That is the time to grab him and point him in the right direction. You three will find a way."

Instinctively, Cathy leaned over the table and firmly grasped Cameron's lower arm. Staring at Cameron she said, "It's good to have you back." She squeezed his arm, then let go. Her meaning was obvious to all at the table. Bad accidents rarely happened to Heart People. Joy was the basis of their daily lives. Cameron's accident stood out a mile. He was highly respected, not that he was aware of it. He was also closely observed, and it became clear when he had surfaced from his mourning, to the relief of those around him.

Cameron looked at the faces around the table and said to them, "Oh, it's good to be back."

The Heart Voyance School

4

Lower Slaughter

Xhio stood on a bridge above a small stream, his ponderings disturbed as he turned and watched the small man saunter through the village towards him, his stick held in his right hand, supporting his weakened leg. Even in his prime, Marcus de Brey would have never been considered a tall man, and in the latter half of life, his frame just seemed to be getting absurdly thin. His thin grey/black hair hung straight down, cut off just below the ears. Everyone here dressed expensively, but the way Marcus was attired expressed a refined style, which only the rich French seemed to be able to achieve.

It was Marcus who had called an emergency meeting of the Twelve to discuss the latest report from Professor Beck. The new patent application of a free energy machine from England was the catastrophe they had been waiting for. Professor Beck, of course, did not believe such a thing was possible. But Marcus knew better. The machine threatened their power structures and therefore their reason for existence. This disaster was not going to be allowed to happen.

Xhio was secretly glad that the focus of the group was England, meaning that they had turned away from the U.S., Xhio's responsibility. His primary focus was on destroying the Christian Circles that were forming there and he did not yet want to report back his failure to crush them. He especially did not want Marcus to know, because if there was one person in the world he might be afraid of, Marcus was that person.

The Christian Circles had been a thorn in his side for a long time now. They had started twenty years earlier. The idea had quickly spread, so that most of the American countryside had a local circle. The concept was quite simple. The Circles were groups of Christians whose primary purpose was to support each other. The members of the Circle tended not to move around, instead staying in one place. They paid off their mortgages. Then they did something that for Xhio was unfathomable: they started paying off each other's mortgages. They organized bartering systems to exchange goods without the need for currency. Their focus was not just on themselves but also on their immediate neighbors, regardless of religion or creed. If your child was ill, a stranger would get in contact, advising which doctor to go to. You did not have to pay money for the doctor; you paid in kind through the bartering system at your own pace. Sooner or later whole neighborhoods joined in, each willing to give their skills for free. Their cooperation started to deepen and they found new ways of doing things: a carpenter and an electrician got together and patented a new method of wiring a wooden house, with the wires being added inside the wooden beams before the wood even left the yard, halving the wiring costs by the unique way the electric joint had been added to the wood. The patent was offered for free to all Christian circles, the rest of the country paying a small fee. In this way the Circles brought in outside finance, which supported their whole effort of "togetherness".

All this was taking them off the financial grid and hence out of the control of the Twelve. Once they were free of debt as a group, they could do what they wanted and were difficult to influence. Xhio's assignment was to bring the Christian Circles under control. At first he had thought it would be easy. Fear was the great manipulator. The classic strategy of sending in charismatic church leaders to preach against the Circles did not work. The Circle members just left the sermonizing churches, taking half the congregation with them. They all belonged to multiple different churches anyway, so it was not difficult for them to find new places to worship which were not so dogmatic. Sending in uncouth ex-cons to create a scandal did not work either. The Circles seemed to have a good understanding of whom they could influence for the good and who was pure trouble. So far they had stayed away from trouble. They had made themselves immune from the two biggest fears - survival of the individual and survival of their society.

Now the Christian Circles wanted to widen their connectivity. They and the Muslim Circles were co-operating with each other, creating a network of understanding they called the "Alliance for God."

Xhio's problem had become even bigger. The more he learnt about them, the more he began to secretly admire them. They were not telling anyone how to live their lives. They never preached hell and damnation, they were simply trying to create loving communities. By not tying themselves down to a career to pay back big mortgages, they freed up so much of their time and energy for community work that they were succeeding too. They listened hard to the sound of, "We" and lost interest as soon as anyone mentioned "Us and Them". Wasn't this just the sort of community that a mature humanity would start to create? Did the Twelve really need to attack it or had they become so institutionalized themselves that they were reacting out of habit rather than for humanity's good? It was no wonder that Xhio had difficulties destroying Christian Circles. His heart was not in it.

Until today, he had believed that he was the only one with problems. Each of them had their own particular geographical location to look after. His was Northern America, de Brey had Africa, Sir Robert McKinsey had the U.K. and Russia, Tommasi European Union, Mistry India, Yang China, etc. Their goal was to keep control of societies, making sure they did not rise above a certain level of consciousness, where changes in humankind would then become dangerous. The dumbing down of populations during the second half of the twentieth century had been an easy outcome for their predecessors. Now, however, things were different. Great swathes of the masses could no longer be controlled with fear of war and terror. And now, their last hope of financial and energy servitude seemed to have been overcome as well.

Looking round at the table this morning, he read a great deal between the lines. Nearly all of them had problems with the communities living in the countryside, although few had yet had the courage to openly say so. Tommasi was struggling with a European Union where referendums were easy to call and quickly set in law, circumnavigating central governmental control. This was a subject no longer discussed after the latest disaster of obtuse financial restrictions, brought in through a referendum. This lack of openness amongst them was hindering their current discussions. There was "an elephant in the room" but no one was mentioning it. There was too much left unsaid.

They had just been having a break in the meeting. Their discussions were going round in circles and it was clear to Xhio that Marcus was getting more and more impatient. His French nature was normally comfortable in this Anglo-Saxon dominated culture, but today was an exception. Here they were, the twelve most powerful men in the whole world, and they couldn't even agree on what the problem was. Xhio was also astonished. Indecision here? Could it be that they had lost their purpose?

He looked up at the surrounding hills. All around would be top security, with no one entering or leaving the village without central control knowing about it. As usual, there was not a single security guard in sight. He was proud of the fact that their personal security team was so much more effective than any police force or secret service team.

Inside the hotel, all the rooms were booked for the meeting, so there were no other guests to bother them. Yesterday afternoon, three teenagers on bicycles had stopped off at the hotel and stayed in the bar for a drink. Before they had even sat down their names were already known, and they were given an all clear status. Not bad considering that this meeting had been set up at such short notice.

As soon as he noticed Xhio, Marcus de Brey headed in his direction. "This isn't working," he said. "If we let an unlimited energy supply become widespread with everyone able to generate more than enough energy for themselves, we will not be able to control anything anymore. The world is slipping out of our command and we cannot even agree on what, if anything, the symptoms are," said Marcus.

Xhio nodded gently while continuing to stare down at the stream. He took his time before replying. "So what would you suggest we do?"

Marcus looked up and around, taking in the details of the whole village before turning to face Xhio. "Sir Robert did well to find this village for our meeting. Lower Slaughter, what an inspiring name. We have always taken the high ground, controlling the strategies of governments in the long term, directing the media, using banks to great effect. Now perhaps it is more efficient to take the lower ground, set policies in motion that will restrict these communities, hitting back at the new education initiatives which have developed. Bring them back under government control. Let's fight the lower battle, the lower slaughter."

Xhio looked at Marcus, neither one of them displaying any sign of emotion. "That is how you succeed in Africa. But here? Not without the risk of a backlash. For me it would not be possible. Americans are too cautious about government interfering with the rights of an individual. And since the Haig affair, no government would be willing to try such tactics. It would be political suicide."

Marcus looked straight back at him. "Then we must move forward where we can. The English can take their punishment lying down as they always have. Perhaps the U.S. will be more amenable when they see the rest of the world progressing in one direction. Where one country is moving out of control too fast we will hit harder. Where the country is moving along as planned, we can leave it alone. We can hammer out an agreement that we all can follow."

Xhio nodded to him and thought it through. The rest of them would go along with it. Marcus de Brey was the most reactionary of all of them and this last-ditch effort would buy them some more time. He now thought it obvious that the world was changing and there was little they could do to stop it. If one group managed to invent free energy machines, it would not be long before another group managed it. The Twelve had always known that sooner or later it would come to this. The others wanted a more reasonable approach. Now if Marcus stuck his neck out pursuing this strategy, there would be plenty of candidates to chop it off if he failed. The World might be a better place if Marcus lost face in the Twelve. So either way this strategy had its advantages. Xhio gave a small smile and said, "Let's go back and try it."

5

Do You Believe?

Elaine looked to the left at the administration building. From here she could see through the large windows to the people inside going up and down the spiral staircase. Funny, she always thought of them all busy sitting at their desks, but here they were running up and down as if it was a new form of exercise.

She was sitting on a bench in the schoolyard, swinging her legs back and forth. Elaine was too large for the bench so it took some maneuvering to get her legs to swing at all. Instead of swinging them straight, she had to swing them at a diagonal, and then one after another rather than together, so they formed an X as they went forwards and back.

The new teacher came out of the building and headed towards Elaine. Mrs. Graves, although doubtless she would call herself Melody. She had nice eyes and would be almost likeable if she wasn't married to that bully. Elaine had seen Mr. Graves only once at a school event but that was all she needed. He reminded her of too many animal-men she had known while she was growing up in London. What did Melody ever see in him?

"So you're taking me to the inquisition?" piped in Elaine before any false politeness could start up.

"Yes, I have just been polishing the rack and making sure that the wood was organic. It wouldn't be doing for the parents to be complaining that the instruments of torture were made out of poisonous raw materials, would it?" Elaine did well to hide her astonishment. Most of the teachers from her old school seemed to have forgotten what a sense of humor was, never mind use it on a student. This might turn out to be fun after all. Perhaps she had misjudged this situation - you don't joke with the person you are about to kick out of school, so perhaps they were thinking of letting her stay after all.

Elaine followed Melody into the building, up the staircase and into a small room, where Cameron was waiting for them. The walls were colored in a light green, with a deep red carpet, and the room gave off a very warm feeling. There was an easy chair opposite a two-seat sofa, and a small irregular five-sided table in the centre of the room. Cameron rose up and put a hand out to greet her. He had a warm smile, which lit up his face. She smiled back hesitantly.

"I'm sorry, I've not had much of a chance to talk to you since you came here."

"Too busy playing Truthsayer with the police, I expect," riposted Elaine. She sat down in the single easy chair. Cameron and Melody hesitated, then both sat down on the sofa together, being careful to keep some distance from each other, without being ill-mannered. There was tension there.

"I've been doing the year end accounts if my memory is to be trusted," replied Cameron.

"Since when is the memory of a Truthsayer not to be trusted?"

Cameron laughed. "Truthsayers do not need their own memories to do that work. But that isn't why we are here. Ms Graves here has recently joined the teaching staff. The teachers have been wondering how you are settling in?"

"Is that some sort of polite speak for "interrogate the little witch "cos we can't work with her anymore?""

"Yes," replied Cameron and grinned at her. Elaine grinned back. Melody also smiled and settled back into the sofa.

"What's up, Elaine? You wanted to come here but you seem to have grown more dissatisfied as the days wore on. Why don't you tell me what's been going on in your world."

"Well … it was okay at first. The people are nice and the school is dead pretty. It's just …" Elaine's voice dried up and did not continue. She looked down at the floor.

"Tell me what you were expecting it to be like before you came here?" asked Melody.

Elaine hesitated before starting. "Well, I was picturing a mystery school and that means mysterious. I was expecting to meet all sorts of weird and wacky people. Students who kept seeing things and who talked about what all the wonderful things invisible spirits were telling them. You were going to teach me how to see those things and how to meditate and how to, well, lots of other stuff. Instead all I get is geography and mathematics and *more* mathematics and a bit more art and it's all really nice, but what's it all for? And the others, I asked them, I went to all those who I thought would know, the ones who were different, you know, like flying on a different planet. I asked them what they saw. They just didn't reply. I thought they were being shy but after I asked a few more, I realized that they were not saying anything about what they could see, because they couldn't see. And then I just thought, what's the point, what am I doing here anyway? This place is so useless even my parents would be better than this."

Cameron just grinned at her. "We do things differently here."

Elaine's face lightened up a little and a small smile composed itself.

"In the upper school we begin to tell the students how it works. If we tell Elaine now, perhaps that would help her understand what she is learning here?" said Melody.

Cameron's eyes caught Melody's and an almost imperceptible nod went between them. They were going to be telling Elaine one of the most important things of her life. They were not certain she would be able to take it in.

Cameron took a deep breath. "Okay, let's take a big step back in time. Way back in time, to the beginning of the Earth as we perceive it. This was the first period of time. Everything was solid rock and water. No plant life. A pretty dull place all-in-all. Then came the second period of time. Plant life started. The Earth became green. With the establishment of the seasons the plants grew and gained a rhythm, blossoming in spring and dying in the autumn. Next came the animals. And with them the third period. They grew and diversified. We ended up with a whole range of various animals."

Elaine yawned. "So?"

Cameron grinned back at her, "With the fourth period, humankind appeared, the final phase of the Earth's development."

"Are you telling me I am here to learn how to create the Earth?"

Cameron and Melody began to relax a little. "No, some big Creator has gone and done that for you. Humans are also Creators though. We create the physical environment around us - the buildings, schools, the roads and fields. So for example, we build houses that suit our needs. That is one thing type of thing we create. Another thing we create is done with our minds. Our thoughts and emotions are things we create, our thoughts are particularly important. How to structure our thoughts, that's what we teach here."

Elaine looked puzzled. "What do you mean?"

"Thoughts can have a structure. That is the basis of rhetoric, logic and philosophy. But there are many different ways of putting your thoughts together. You will learn more about these in the upper school. What we teach here is a way of thinking which follows the same principle as the Creator's thought, as I just outlined."

Melody leaned forward and took over, "What Cameron said about the Earth, we have here in the physical domain, plant life, animals and humans. That is how the world was designed. The earth is just a thought in the great Creator's Mind. So following the qualities of the things the creator made, in the order they were created, tells us about the structure of Divine thought. What we do is to follow that same thought process through. That way we start thinking in the same style as the Creator rather than just putting thoughts together any old how.

"So whenever we think of what to teach in a lesson, we think of the various qualities of what we want to say and divide it up into these four categories, earth, plant life, animal and human. Then the lesson will get taught in these four parts, one after another, in order. In this way the lesson is taught in the same manner in which the world was created."

Elaine looked up at the window, silently thinking to herself. Melody and Cameron sat still watching her.

"Is that all there is to it? You built a whole school just to teach that?"

Cameron smiled calmly. "No. There is more to it than that, but those are the basics. This way of training your thoughts is like putting bread in a toaster - it lines up the thoughts so that they are all pointing the same way. Normal thought is all higgledy-piggledy and its chaos stops intuitions from reaching you. Intellectual thought is structured but tends to block intuition. By lining up your thoughts in this way, the intuitions can flow through. It means you can be both highly intuitive and very logical at the same time. It enables us to unite the left and right brain activities in a harmonious way."

"So you have a normal education," continued Melody, "but hidden within that is a subtle way of thinking which you are practicing all the time. We do a great deal of consciousness lessons later on in the upper school, which we think is a more appropriate time for such things. For now you will still have concentration exercises and a few other delicacies to keep you going for the delights of the later years!'

Elaine was now looking down at the table, the fingers of her right hand twirling her hair. From the movements on her cheek it was clear that she was nibbling the inside of her mouth with her teeth.

"Well, it's just, you know…" she said.

"Just ask," said Melody.

"Okay. I know it's off topic. But the others were talking about "Branching' and I didn't know what it was. It sounded kind of important and I hated not knowing."

Cameron and Melody turned to each other again. It was clear from their expressions that they had no problems talking further. They both relaxed further into the sofa.

"There's a whole view on history that you have not had in your previous school, most of which has to do with the development of consciousness," said Cameron. "There was an event that happened just over thirty years ago. As far as we are aware it is Unique in the history of humanity, and we call it the Branching. This is not easy to say. It's been a while since I tried to explain it…"

"Let me try," interrupted Melody. "I remember what my parents told me about it." She leaned forward towards Elaine as she began to talk.

"For all those living then, it was a single event, a moment in time when there was a pivotal instant. My parents told me this.

"For my Mum it was simple. She was looking out the window on a brilliant sunny day and she suddenly felt a deep oneness with the world, a profound inner joy, which never left her. This gave her a sense of security and confidence that enabled her personality to steadily develop over the following years.

"For my father, it was different. He was asked a question. Do you want to know what the question was?"

"Go on," said Elaine.

"He was traveling on a bus at the time. He said he felt that a question came from outside. The question that he was asked was, 'Do you believe in all that is good in the world?'"

Elaine watched Melody's face, waiting for her to continue. "Is that all?" she asked.

Melody and Cameron looked at each other. "It's sort of the central question to ask," said Cameron.

"It had a tremendous effect on my father," continued Melody. "He thought about all the good in the world for a second. By focusing on it he realized that not only did he believe in it, he wanted to identify with it. This identification or connectedness to good never left him, he cantered his life on it. This conscious connection with good was the pivot, that which sent his life in a new direction. That was when the changes began."

"When did this happen?" asked Elaine.

"It would be about two years before the Tin Can Riots," answered Cameron.

"Do you mean to say you don't know the exact date?" asked Elaine.

"It seemed that for different people it was on different dates, we guess spread across a week in all. Then in all the confusion ...'

"What confusion?" asked Elaine.

"Well, this had a randomness to it. Families were split down the middle. Some had this experience, for others it was just another day. Or week. Just no difference. It took a while to figure out. The new people were very concerned about their fellow humans around them but could not get them out of their reverie. They tried talking about it but then found out that many hadn't a clue what they were talking about. So they were christened the Sleepers, because it seemed as if they had just slept through this great time of change. The others go under several different names in different communities but here we call them Heart People.

"The Heart People then started the Exodus..."

They were interrupted by a sudden knock at the door. Joel burst through without waiting for an answer. "Cameron, the government is going to close the school down. You have to come now."

Cameron looked over at Elaine, "We have not finished. Will you wait for us?"

Elaine looked across at Cameron and then at Melody. "I want to talk to you both together again. I'll hold out for that."

6

V-Gen Installation

The cellar steps were solid concrete, with one straight flight down bringing you to the small entrance room with three doors off it. Only two of the school buildings had been built with cellars, as luck would have it, at opposite ends of the schoolyard.

It was late afternoon a few weeks later as Cameron knocked on the door to his left. He entered straight away. The room inside was large and contained all the utility machines for the school in a clear, well-maintained space. To his left was the electrical equipment, with the thick cables from the solar panels on the roofs of the buildings coming down into one central metallic box, which sorted out which electricity to use from which source. To the right were the water tanks, some for collecting rainwater from the roofs. One tall metal box was for coolant, which was used to extract heat from the earth after being pumped a hundred meters vertically into the ground. The latest collections of units were smaller heat exchange boxes, which created an audible humming noise. Many of the south facing walls of the school had been removed and replaced with exchange windows. The exchange windows were clear but had multiple layers to them including one where liquid absorbed the heat from the sun's rays and was transferred down to the cellar to be used in the school's water heating system. In all the school could generate seventy percent of its energy requirements. Now all of this was about to change. The school was about to move into energy surplus.

In the centre of the room was a round container standing about one and a half meters high. The container was in three parts. Above, a funnel-shaped piece of copper, flat on top and almost to a point at the lower end, looking like a human head on a neck. In the middle, a circular copper piece, almost perfectly round and about one meter in diameter. At the bottom, a steel box shape. A man with long, grey dreadlocks tied back in a bun and dressed in blue dungarees, was working on connecting a series of pipes and cables to the steel box part of the machine.

"Hi, I'm Cameron, the administrator here. I just wanted to check that you have all you need."

The man looked up, his face broadening into a round smile. "Kurt's the name, Installator extraordinaire. Another hour, then it's all connected up. You have so much of the necessary infrastructure already here, it's been a cinch. A couple of hours admiring this machine in action, what you might call testing, then I'm done."

Cameron recognized the voice and peered at him. "You're one of the college professors, aren't you?"

"Yeah, I picked up that title as well. Before I went into the wonderful world of intuition academia, I wandered from job to job, trying to decide what I wanted to do. Along the way I picked up qualifications as a plumber and electrician. It was while I was an electrician that I decided I wanted to study and be able to build hi-tech gadgets instead of just following a set of instructions to install them. Then I got landed in this heart consciousness malarkey. My background helped in the design of the V-Gen. It was like I was made for the job. I could ensure from the beginning that the first prototype was safe and an easy install. I do the first test installations like this one. It gets me out of the office and round the country to a few interesting places and a couple of good pubs. Felt a bit like old times, you know."

They grinned at each other for a second before Kurt returned to adjusting some screws on the V-Gen. "Hey Cameron, you can give me a hand if you've got a mo'. Just flick that mains switch on and off when I tell you."

Cameron walked across to where Kurt was pointing, to two new electrical boxes attached to one wall. There were two electric cables running from the V-Gen across to the main electrical switches against one wall. Both cables were black and about as thick as a young child's arm. "If you flick that top switch when I give you the nod, we can see how well this runs. If I start twitching and sparks are flying, then switch it off again, eh?"

When Cameron moved the mains switch, Kurt busied himself with the control panel of the V-Gen, a simple touch screen on the side of the machine. Shortly it sprang into life, with a satisfied sigh from Kurt. The machine began to rock slightly from side to side. As Kurt made more adjustments, the machine seemed to speed up, the rocking stopped and a quiet humming sound could be heard as the machine made an infinitesimal vibration.

"Now let's see how much juice this tin box can generate." Kurt went across to the mains connection and looked at the electronic dials there. Cameron followed his gaze and listened to the forthcoming explanation. "Here is the normal measurement of how much electricity we are pulling off the grid. This newer dial over here measures how much electricity we are putting back into the mains, with the V-Gen and some of your solar panels. As you can see it's already feeding into the grid. I've already looked through your electricity bills to see how much you use and I've set the machine for about a quarter of that. I'll look tomorrow to see how much electricity you use and how much we are generating, but I suspect that at this time of year we are going to be generating more than we need."

"Does that mean we can vary the amount of electricity we can produce?" asked Cameron.

"This little baby could generate ten times what this school needs and could easily be used to keep all the staff, pupils and families supplied with free energy. Perhaps the whole town. However, we are keeping the output low for the minute. There is only permission to install a few test devices and it wouldn't do to awaken the anger of the generating companies by frying their power cables with so much juice, that they start screaming that their long term future is in mortal danger. Those guys and gals can scream pretty loud and they know which ears to scream in to try and stop us."

"So we keep the output low enough so that they won't notice?" asked Cameron.

Kurt started packing some of his tools in his small tool box. "Oh they'll notice alright, they will be monitoring all the test installations whether we have given them permission to or not. However, we decided to keep the outputs from these babies low so that the power companies are not over excited about them and are left thinking that they are only producing a little more energy than they use. Once we are patented and have clarified the legal issues, then we will start switching on some of the Big Daddies."

"You have bigger machines?" asked Cameron.

"Buy me a pint and I'll tell ya," grinned Kurt.

An hour later Cameron was sitting in 'Ye Olde Nags Head' pub, with two empty glasses of beer on the table in front of him. Kurt was standing at the bar and had just finished paying for the next round of drinks. He walked the short distance back to the table carrying the two pints of beer. Sitting down he looked around and said, "Nice place this. Don't look much from the outside but it's dead cosy and oldie worldie. I love pubs with low ceilings "n' big fireplaces. Even these chairs look as if they could be a hundred years old. Cheers!"

They drank from their second beer. "It's authentic though, not plastic," said Cameron. "This place has been a pub or an inn for about four hundred years. So the old feeling it gives off is real."

"I thought you school people didn't drink, strict teetotal, like?" asked Kurt.

"Most of us don't drink," replied Cameron. "Meditation and alcohol are not a good mix. One tends to make you more conscious and calm, the other tends to get you depressive and egoistic. Alcohol affects different people in different ways though and if I only have one or two drinks every now and again then it has little effect on me. The day after a drink

I'm a little out of kilter, slightly more irritable in my thoughts but nothing that comes to expression. But I haven't had a beer for a long time, so I thought, well, why not?"

"Wow, you must be pretty good at observing yourself. There are guys around the college who are also like that, but also a few other techie experts like me who aren't yet that strong on self observation. Being in the college is a great change from being in a city university. I really like it there and feel quite at home. It's a different culture, it has a supporting rather than a back-stabbing atmosphere. And they seem to better understand my ability to find answers quickly.

"Say, back when you visited us at the college two years ago, didn't you bring your wife along? You traveled all the way on yer bike from what I remember! Is she going to join us tonight? She is a beauty next to us dead beats!"

Cameron's face froze. He opened his mouth but no words came out. After a few seconds his head dropped and he looked down at the floor. Kurt's face quickly developed a puzzled expression, "Say, you two didn't split up or anything? You looked so in love, I thought it was a done thing you were still together."

Cameron took a swig of his beer, a deep breath and then leaned forward. "You were right, Caroline and I visited the college on our bicycles. We met on a cycling holiday around the Cotswolds, and cycling was something we loved to do. It's about two days ride to the Dales from here and we thought it would be a good laugh to do it by bike. On the way back, we were almost home, flying down a steep hill. Caroline was ahead and as she went round a tight right hand bend, she cut into it, going further into the middle of the road. There was a lorry coming the other way and he had swung out to get round the tight bend. They didn't see each other. Caroline got caught by the side of the lorry. She didn't stand a chance."

"God, I'm sorry." Kurt's face fell. "Just after your visit I went on holiday, so I didn't get to hear. I'm…"

"It's been over two years now and I'm beginning to lighten up again. This spring was the first that I've noticed since the accident. I'd forgotten what it was like to see the blooms appear and rejoice at the colors and the first promise of sunny days." Cameron paused, supping from his beer and gazing at the fireplace. "For a long time you see, it was like I was walking round in a dark fog and the subtle sweet things in life just passed me by. During that time I also switched roles at school, becoming the school administrator. I couldn't teach the children any more. You have to be fully present in the classroom and I was walking round in this cloud. The children were not learning anything in class and I just didn't take any notice. It's funny, it's only now that I am beginning to feel alive again. I can enjoy the taste of a pint without worrying that I am about to begin drowning my sorrows in a sea of empty pint pots.

"I've never been back on a bicycle though. It's something I couldn't face. The very idea of getting on a saddle again fills me with the desire to vomit. It's a pity, I used to love touring through the countryside. I guess I'm not yet ready for it."

There was a moment of quiet camaraderie between them. They sat back and became aware of the hum of the conversations at the tables around them.

Kurt resumed his previous jolly tone. "You know, one of the things that's different about the college is how we're taught to observe situations. Just being aware of your current surroundings, what's the atmosphere in rooms and between groups of people. Later on it's looking at the bigger stuff, how some projects work out and others don't and trying to recognize the key places where things go wrong or right. We're always taught to go with the flow and how to get things to flow.

"Look at the situation with the V-Gens. It's clear that everything at the Patent Office is blocked. For a project in flow, this is more like a desert stream than a river, ain't no flow, absolute no go, d'you know what I mean?"

Kurt stopped and took a swig of his beer while waiting for Cameron to respond.

"We've solved the energy problems of the world but in a way that current day science will find hard to understand, and therefore accept. The machine is very hard to comprehend from a traditional scientific viewpoint. Given the fact that nearly all the energy and oil businesses face extinction within ten years as a direct result of this invention, it was always going to be an uphill struggle to get it mainstream. Those monster businesses are going to fight for survival. But we didn't expect to get stuck before we'd even got a patent. This is quite exceptional."

"It's just the start," Kurt went on. "Things will continue this way every time we make a move forward. We had problems elsewhere too. We shipped out parts for a big machine to be assembled in Texas, just the bits they can't make themselves yet. It took ages to get through customs. Admittedly the parts are strange and it's a bad joke to say, yes we are making a machine which will provide power for half of Texas. Your credibility is put into question."

"Half of Texas?" asked Cameron.

"Told you, the V-gen is incredible! Yeah well, we thought Texas, they love big concepts, so we'll give them one. It might be where the oil companies are strong but it also has two big cities which are short of water, and the biggest cost of desalination plants is…"

"Energy. You've got them by the short 'n' curlies."

"Yep. Except we want to give it away, almost for free. But someone has also got us by the short and curlies too, otherwise we would not be hampered so much. We've either got to find a different approach or we've got to find the key log," said Kurt.

"The key log?" asked Cameron.

"Traditionally, lumberjacks used to cut down trees and then put all the tree trunks, the logs, into the rivers to let the water transport them down to the towns. Every so often the logs would jam together and get stuck. But there was always one log, if you moved it, it freed up all the others, so they all started flowing downstream again. Someone has created a log jam for us. Once we are through the patent problem we'll be hit by the next blockage. And so on. It just won't stop. Somehow we need to find the one thing, which will change everything and remove all the blockages at one go. That is the key log."

"So how do we go about finding it?" muttered Cameron.

"That's what I thought you intuition chaps and chapesses would be good at," said Kurt, grinning.

Cameron looked at the fire, his head tilted to one side, lost in thought. He looked up at Kurt "We've been so caught up in how to defend our schools against the new education policy that we haven't given the V-Gen much thought."

"Yeah, you've got another log in the jam there. Got you caught reet good, haven't they? Key log, find your key log."

Cameron looked back at the fireplace. Where is the key log? One thing was for sure. The schools were being attacked because they had invented the V-Gen machines. The V-Gen machines were not being attacked because of the schools. The key log was somewhere out there with the powers of the world. It was intuitively clear to Cameron that the key log was going to be one particular person as well. Someone who wanted to hold onto their reins of power and stop the world gaining free energy. The schools were now being challenged to come out of their safe world and interact with the Sleepers' world. This was something they were not used to. The last person who had represented the Schools to the public was him. He was likely to play a key role in this situation too. But in addition to public relations, there was this second task for the school, to find out who was trying to kill off the V-gen machines. How was he going to find that one person who could change everything? And how was he going to neutralize their power? He did not know how. But he was looking forward to working it out.

7

Mole at Work

Mole walked into his "Machine Room". He was a tall man, well built and in his mid-fifties. His receding hairline left a surrounding head of thick grey hair. His large muscular frame had gained a widening midrift in his later years. He looked around at the morning sunshine beamed through the glass wall of the room. Someone, he couldn't remember who, had installed a sophisticated sun screen, using a beam of light to activate sensitive plasma coated on to the window panes. The light beam was programmed to switch on when the sun shone, charging the plasma to block out the sun's rays and at the same time projecting a picture into the room. Currently it was van Gogh's "Sunflowers" displaying from the top of the windows, whilst the lower half, untouched by direct sunlight, was still showing the outside landscape.

Inside, on an array of chaotically arranged large green glass tables was an assortment of screens and mikes which perhaps looked the same as in any international bank in London. What was functioning behind these interfaces however was some of the most powerful equipment Mole could get his hands on. Not all of it was legal.

On the white washed wall facing the large window, there was a small dent just below shoulder height, where he had once lost his temper and thrown a punch at the wall. Next to the dent, someone had hit the wall with a small hand axe, leaving the axe embedded in the wall. This was a typical comment from the crew, which seemed to say: if you are going to hit something, do it properly.

No one else was there at the minute. At busy times of the night, there could be ten or more people in the room, all of them sophisticated Net hackers who came here to pursue their anti-establishment goals. However, at nine o'clock in the morning, most of them were sleeping off their hard night's work.

Hard work it was. They had come together to inflict revenge. The latest government wanted to bring back fingerprint tracing, the ability to track anyone's activities throughout the Net. This had been made illegal twenty-five years ago due to gross misconduct by secret services, who spent more time tracking alternative benign political groups than terrorist organizations. Not that Mole was a great believer in the anger of terrorist organizations; it was the mad individuals that presented a greater danger to society as far as he was concerned.

He had come in early to ponder his biggest problem. As Mole, it was not difficult for him to penetrate into almost any Com he wished. Even the most secure machines just needed time before he found his way in. With most of the government's machines it had been too easy. When he was a member of the establishment he had left so many subtle cuts in the safety nets, it was a triviality for him to creep through into the "Top Secret" archives. There he and the crew - they called themselves the Cleaners - had managed to find paths through the whole of the government organization, into every database they could get their hands on. They now had a good view of how much data was kept on every citizen.

Lucky for the citizens of the United Kingdom, the government was too inefficient to have webbed all their data together. Otherwise, a complete picture of every move every citizen made would be available to anyone who had access. Currently only the Cleaners and the spies had the complete overview of everything that was stored.

Why did the government need breakdowns of the average weekly shopping trolley of every adult? Or how much money went in and out of every bank account every month, not that the tax department even knew such figures existed! Most of it was collected, summarized, stored and rarely used. Mole did give them some credit - not all of the data was public knowledge and it was obvious that many of the databases were seldom touched, so there was no evidence that other Hackers like the Cleaners had ever gained access to this before.

Mole's dislike of government control knew no bounds. It ran deep in his soul. He knew what he wanted to do with this information. This was a minefield, which with just one explosion could be used to damage the government. He did not just want to damage it though; he wanted to destroy it. Or to be more precise, he wanted to destroy the person who had brought him down. And if he brought down a whole corrupt government at the same time, he was not going to loose sleep over it. He was not going to ruin himself in the process though, so how was he going to proceed? Revenge was going to be a well-prepared dish.

Snowy came in, rattling the door handle, half opening, half-kicking the door before slamming it shut with a flick of his boots. He was dressed in his usual black leather jacket, black jeans and black t-shirt, the whole gloomy ensemble in a weird contrast to his pure white hair and permanent cheeky grin of youth.

"Watchya, Molie, how's it tickin'?"

Mole grinned back at him, "I didn't expect you in this early. What are you up to?"

Snowy went across to one of the desks, talking as he began to interact with the terminal there, looking between the terminal and Mole. "Caught a look at them Golden Coffins last night and figgered 'em out a bit more. Neat set-up. I picked the one in France "n' tried bouncin' signals their way for a couple of hours but got nuffin'. Then I realized there weren't no signals comin' out either. What's in the air, I thought? Then it got to me - they ain't usin' no wireless, bugger all, they must be stuck on landlines. So I did an ancient data match, looking at what lines there were in the area and matching them to house addresses. Didn't take long "cos their village is so small and most are using wireless "Net anyway. Looks like our French Golden Coffin has one line in through a dedicated server, just for themselves. They've got lotsa power there but only a trickle of input/output. Leaves it pretty vulnerable to snoopin'. It got to be late last night when I found this out, so I put a recorder on the line so we can review all their stuff and also put some searches out on the other Coffins, see if they have the same set-up or not. Cool, eh?"

Mole had by this time stopped working and was concentrating on what Snowy had said. "God, that's brilliant, Snowy. If we can monitor all their traffic we can soon crack 'em open." Mole dwelt on the latest news. The Golden Coffins were something they had been trying to crack for a long time. They had discovered them by chance one day when chasing up who was sending influential emails to key decision makers in the British government. The emails were always short and cryptic, but the change in policy afterwards was unmistakable. Over time they had found several other sources of such emails, all from sites where they discovered the owners were exceedingly wealthy. That, together with the fact that their traffic was so low, soon earned them the title of Golden Coffins, the very rich whose Net activity was so low they appeared to be lifeless. The Golden Dead, in their Golden Coffins with their Gold Coffers.

Having one landline in and out was a weakness in their security though. Once they could start monitoring the IO it was only a matter of time before they discovered what encryption techniques were being used. Then they were ripe to be cracked open.

"How many Coffins are you searching for, Snowy?"

"All twelve, Molie, runnin' fine. We're going to crack 'em, ain't we?" grinned Snowy.

"Oh yes, we can start a countdown. Their time is running out."

"Summit else - did you see that they all got together in a hotel not so far from Oxford? They're there right now. Odd, 'cos they only met three months back. Wot's got 'em so strung up that they have ter meet? Not like them, is it, not a chatty bunch of bananas at the best o' times eh? So wot's buggin' 'em?"

"Snowy, they're running scared of something. Let's get some more help on this. Years ago in my misspent youth I was a member of an international group of Hackers. We went by various different names, the Green Knights Templar, the Great Swords, the Grey Shadows, but mostly the Green Knights."

Snowy looked across and grinned, "Hey, even I heard o' them."

"Well, that was us. We became very close and trusting. We don't contact much nowadays but the Golden Coffins were a theme for us back then as well. The Dead don't get to meet regularly so if they are meeting now they must be shaken up about something. It's unusual for them to even allow their dirty doings to appear on the Net. I want to take it to the Green Knights. All this new info is your find, can I tell them about it?"

By this time Snowy had given up all pretence of working at the computer. "Who we talkin' about?"

"Well, the only famous ones are Suki Su in the States and Shark Manifesto in Germany. You will have heard of them?" Mole was smiling now. He had known Snowy for several years but this was the first time he had trusted him with a story from his well-spent youth.

"Heard? That's like askin' have I heard of Billie Holiday and Elvis Presley? Hey Molie, I didn't know you knew such Legends, roll on, it would be mucha cool for them to start singin' with my new news about the Coffins. Go ahead, Molie, yer makin' my day!"

"Notable, Snowy! I'll get on with it. Suki and Shark are easy to contact, the rest should not be hard to find."

"They don't spend all their time online, what they doin' now?"

"Suki spends most of her time acting as a go between, trying to connect different groups up. It's her who got the Muslim Circles and the Christian Circles to form an alliance. Shark runs a half-way house in Hamburg."

"Wot's a half-way house?"

"It was an idea we had about fifteen years ago. There are plenty of people in the cities who are looking for another way of life but who are not yet ready to jump into one of the societies you can find outside the Domes. So we set up houses or buildings inside the Domes where you can enjoy a lighter atmosphere and get to meet with other Fringe People, as we call them. Shark has a building in Hamburg. It acts as a community centre for the local alternatives there, lots of German punks, Goths, Cobblers 'n' so on. He does a great job, even if it is sometimes quite difficult. The Cobblers in particular are quite prone to violence and that is something hard for a heart-person to be around. It causes an ache in the heart, which seems to last for days. That's really tough for Shark."

Talking about being in a Dome brought back memories. Mole had grown up in the countryside, so working in the government buildings in Westminster had been stifling. Sometimes it felt like you were going to choke to death in there on the energy pollution. Weekends away were a must, the only way he could survive. It was obvious to him why the Government went so astray, in that atmosphere they could do little else.

Well, if there was one thing that appealed to Mole more than hurting governments, it was having a go at those behind the governments and the people in the Golden Coffins were exactly that sort of people. Now he was going to get his chance to get his own back. He was going to enjoy this.

8

Watching the Sunset

Cameron signed the last piece of paper, at long last clearing his desk. He was glad to have finished. He felt as if he had spent all day just pushing pieces of paper around. He had saved up all the documents that needed signing and now he had completed them. It still amused him how much paper administration was needed to run a school.

Melody walked in and smiled at him. "Do you have time to talk about Elaine?"

Cameron thought for a moment before answering, "I was just ready to leave. I have been in the office all day and could do with a change. Jailed to the office, a prisoner of work! It's a nice evening - how about we walk into the village and get a coffee?"

"If you've been stuck in the office all this time, why don't we walk up to the castle and enjoy the fresh air?" replied Melody.

Cameron agreed. He locked up the office with his ID card and they started walking down the lane, heading for the public footpath up the hillside. He breathed a contented sigh, letting all the tension of the day go. "I like it here in early summer when the flowers in the valleys are in full bloom. There's a quietness about the hills, which soothes the soul. When I feel the wind blowing it's as if all the junk thoughts in my head are being cleansed away."

"You seem so clear headed, people would be surprised to hear you say that." There was a teasing note to Melody's voice as she glanced sideways at him.

"If you knew half the things that go through my mind you might be shocked!" Cameron felt his face blush slightly and hoped it was not visible in the evening colors.

"Elaine has been progressing," said Melody, quickly switching the subject. "Her mood swings are less frequent, and it looks as if she is concentrating more. It is clear she is looking for the thought forms in the lessons but she is often not finding them. Not surprising really, as we haven't told her the full story."

Cameron thought before answering. "How is her contact with others in the class? Is she socializing better?"

"I think she took our comments about the quiet studious types being more likely to have developed themselves a bit too seriously. She has not yet found out who is doing what amongst the students and so is going from one to another. At least she is not ignoring anyone. Have you had any ideas about teaching her more about the intuition process?"

Melody looked across at him. Cameron looked back at her. He had to turn away. He had lost his train of thought in the moment of eye contact.

"We have only told her half the story and that's not good. If she left school now she would be in a mess," Cameron said. "It's time to tell her about the transformation process. We'd better start tomorrow."

They continued walking further. The sunset was just reaching its peak of splendour. The whole sky lit up as each individual soft cloud was caught in the dying colors.

Cameron let out a contented sigh. "Oh it's so good to be outside again. Having the day's work behind me, I recall my night's work, so to speak."

Melody looked inquisitive and said, "Go on."

"I had the strangest dream last night. I've had it repeatedly. It's left me quite puzzled. I can still remember it, despite all the activities of the day."

"Would you like to tell me about it? I'm a good listener." Melody turned and looked at Cameron's face. They had been approaching a bench just at the side of the path, which looked out on the valley below.

The move to sit down at the bench came quite naturally. The surrounding hills flattened off and were often moor, bog land with little growing on them. But on some of the lower hills, adventurous farmers had began to plant fruit trees, trying to take advantage of the changing weather patterns. Your eyes were naturally drawn to the beautiful green valley in front of you and they paused as they took in the view. Once settled, Cameron began to recount his dream.

"I was in a strange room. It had a wooden floor, and three sides of the room had simple wooden panelling, all made out of a light colored bleached wood. On the fourth side the whole wall was made up of French windows, except there didn't seem to be any glass in place. The light coming from the outside through the windows was really bright, much brighter than a sunny day. In the room there was only one piece of furniture, a small wooden table. A figure appeared from outside, a short man, medium build, simply dressed. But this man also shone with a bright white light, centered on his heart. On the one hand he was light. On the other hand he was physical.

"The man was carrying something in a velvet cloth. He put the object down on the table and removed the cloth. Inside was the strangest object. It looked like a skull. But it was almost opaque and the light seemed to shine through it, giving off the same impression as the man, of being physical and light at the same time.

"The man turned and looked at me. The warmth in his face did not hide his power. He began talking to me, although his mouth did not move. He said that the skull was to be found on the earth. It had fallen into the wrong hands and those people were misusing its capabilities. The time was drawing near when the skull would be returned to its true guardian. I was to find the skull and keep it safe until the rightful owner turned up. He gazed at me a while longer and then put the skull back into its cloth. Then he picked it up, turned around and walked back out of the French windows, merging into the light."

Melody had an open attentive expression on her face. "What a story! Do you always have such vivid dreams?"

"I know I dream most nights. Whether I remember the dreams or not goes in phases. There are times in my life when every night I have vivid dreams. My wife used to translate them as I was terrible at interpreting the symbols. I guess I've not had so many dreams recently. Do you know anything about dream symbolism?"

"My knowledge of symbolism is limited, but this dream seems obvious. It's about the lost crystal skulls. There was a legend in ancient Atlantis that, twelve skulls were made out of quartz crystal. The Atlantean priests endowed them with special properties. Each had its own particular ability, and each could provide you with knowledge. Anything. It was as if the skulls knew everything that was going on in the whole of the human realm and had memorized it. Ask them a question and they could give you the answer. They also had a special power together. When they were all brought to one place, then they could do something together that each skull individually could not achieve. What that was, is lost to the legend."

Cameron was deep in thought and his questions took a while to surface. "What's known about these skulls now? Where are they?"

"There were some skulls found by western explorers in Central America in the early twentieth century. Some of these ended up in museums throughout the world, others just disappeared. A few were nineteenth century imitations. Others remain in the hands of the natives of Central America. The New Agers at the end of the twentieth century were very interested in them, but since then they seem to have disappeared from view. I think there is still one in the British Museum. Why don't you check and go take a look at it?"

"That's a good idea. Perhaps after seeing a crystal skull I might just put this dream to rest. What about any others: one particular skull being mislaid or misused by the wrong people, have you ever heard of such a thing?" asked Cameron.

"I've not heard any rumors about that. Having knowledge about everything anyone is doing is extremely powerful and certain types of people would be attracted to that. But it's not exactly a possession that they are going to shout about from the rooftops. It would be kept a secret. For dark deeds in dark corners of the world."

"Ah well, makes trying to find a skull seem as easy as finding a lost ring in a sewage farm," said Cameron.

Melody laughed, "But with your abilities it would be easy. I just wonder what you will be doing next!" Cameron gave her a skeptical glance. "Look", she continued, "this skull would be a real treasure to those who have it. It would not be something they would be moving around. It would be kept in one secure location. So, just get out a map of the world and use your intuition to let you see in which part of the world the skull is. Get a more detailed map of the area you choose and do the same thing there. Keep on going and you'll be able to find the exact building it's in."

"But if this skull was being misused, the current custodians would have high electronic security round it, guard dogs and goodness knows what else. I know nothing about those sorts of things. The only way I could deal with a guard dog would be to pat it on the head, presuming it didn't bite my wrist off in the first place, just for practice." He paused. "Hey, you seem to be taking this very seriously."

"Yes, I am," said Melody. "I don't think the dream happened by accident."

Cameron looked at the horizon and then down at the earth, and sighed. "I will have to think about this one, then. This is off the scale of my life."

Melody gave a quiet laugh. "You are not a normal person. Why do you expect to have a normal dream, let alone a quiet life? With time you'll find out what this is about, and then you will take on this task and you will succeed."

Cameron looked intensely at Melody. "You remind me of a woman I met years ago, in my student days," he said, relaxing into the bench. "One summer I went for a holiday to the continent and ended up in a small hotel in Heidelberg, washing dishes. There was a marvelous woman there who owned it, Frau Ostern, very straightforward in her approach to everything. She was already of retirement age when I met her. She didn't approve of students paying tax, so she paid me in cash and gave me free boarding. Took quite a shine to me.

"I had this odd experience while I was there, which I told her about. On one of my days off, I went on the train to Mannheim. I spent the day there and was waiting at the train station on the platform, for the train back. There were quite a few people waiting for the train, and when I started looking at them, one man turned and faced me. He was standing about ten meters away. He looked at me and smiled, then he stepped towards me. He was small, thin, with the typical dark features of the German-Turkish people. His smile grew in intensity, his eyes seemed to get bigger as he approached and I was mesmerized. The look was so loving, as if he saw me for who I really am, all of me, warts "n' all, and it just didn't matter, he still gazed with this loving countenance. When he got to about four meters away, I couldn't hold his gaze anymore, it was too much, too intense, so I turned and looked along the platform in the opposite direction. When I turned back again, the man was gone. He couldn't have got off the platform without me seeing him, as he would have had to pass me by to get to the stairs. I walked up and down the platform looking at all the waiting passengers but he was not there. He had just vanished. On the train journey back I got to brooding on it. This gaze of lovingness from this complete stranger who disappeared into thin air, so strong, without reason, I could draw only one conclusion. When I got back to the hotel I told Frau Ostern the whole story and ended up saying to her that I had just met God. And she said to me, 'You know Cameron, God does not appear to everyone.'"

"So even as a youngster you always had women telling you what a special man you are! Your wife must have been a very perceptive person."

Cameron frowned, not sure how to react to the mention of his wife, not even sure if he was understanding correctly his own swell of emotions.

Melody pushed further. "You were a very close couple weren't you?"

"Yes we were. We had a fantastic communication. Most of us can do the supermarket test," said Cameron. Melody pulled a frown. "You know," Cameron explained, "you are at the supermarket, you suddenly think of something else to buy, something not on your shopping list, and when you get home your partner had been thinking about needing that exact same item you had just bought on the fly. It's basic telepathy."

"Oh yes," said Melody. She turned her head and looked up at the hills. She had not done the supermarket test.

"Well, Caroline and I used to love doing that. We practiced it, just for a laugh. We then realized something else. It happened when one of us would begin to talk about something and the other one had been thinking about the exact same topic. We were never sure what happened. Did she have the original thought and then I detected her thoughts, or did I have the thought and she detected it? Or maybe the thought came from outside and we both picked it up at the same time! Anyway, we kept at it. It developed into a sort of knowingness. It wasn't just pictures of things that we shared, we could know things between us. It brought us even closer together. We could share this knowingness even when doing other things. It was a special relationship."

"I remember when the accident occurred. It shocked us. You blame yourself for her death. Why?"

Cameron looked back at Melody for a long time. It was a very perceptive question and he was not sure how far he was willing to open up.

"It was my idea. The traveling to the college on the bicycles, it was all my plan. Caroline wasn't so keen. If I had followed her wishes, we would have gone by train. It was one of those moments that you have in a relationship, you just push things through without thinking much about it."

"You have thought about it a lot since then. But it wasn't just the planning of the trip, was it?" By this time Melody was staring back at Cameron, as if her large dark eyes could x-ray his head and penetrate his memories. "You were using telepathy with her when she died."

Cameron stared out at the Mam Tor hill. "That's why I wanted to go cycling. I wanted to see how well our telepathy helped us on our journey. Just how much could we communicate. We were doing so well. It was going to be the beginning of a new life for us. The telepathy gave us an intimate understanding. Caroline was using it on the journey back. She was in the lead and had just gone round one of those tight bends on the road and was just sending me what an exquisite view it was from round the corner. Then suddenly her thoughts went from this amazement at the scenery, to something like a ghastly shock. It was as if someone was screaming in my mind. I braked, having difficulty keeping straight with this devastation in my head. As I came round the corner, I saw what had happened. She was so distracted by telepathically sending me the description of the view, that she didn't react fast enough to get out of the way of the approaching lorry. So it was my fault she died. We had not been practicing our newfound communication long enough and she paid the price."

His eyes were moist. That was not going to stop Melody. "You have no right to blame yourself. It's a stupid way of holding in the pain. Let it go. Let her go. I don't think she deserves such stupidity from you."

The tears started falling down Cameron's face. He did not sob, he just gazed into the distance. After a while, he got out his handkerchief and dabbed his eyes. "Thank you," he said. "I needed that."

Now Cameron looked back at Melody. "Now it's your turn. It takes one to know one. If I have been holding on to a dead guilty connection, you know about that type of relationship too. Is that something you brought with you from your family upbringing? Do you carry it with you now?"

Melody let in a deep breath. "OK. You have never met my husband."

"No, he's not around the community so much. Is there a reason for that?"

"He finds it difficult here. He's a Sleeper."

Cameron's face lost its expression, as if all the muscles had suddenly gone to sleep. "Marriage to a Sleeper is sacred. You are giving him a chance to bootstrap up to our level of consciousness. Where is the comparison with my situation?"

Melody turned and looked at him, holding his gaze as she talked. "It's quite simple. Before I left for the college, he hit me. I went away to gather myself and regain my self-respect. The college was perfect for that. They know how to identify your strengths and demonstrate how good you are. After a while it was clear I was not running away but accomplishing deep learning. But they also made it quite clear that the marriage was empty, I could do no more. The police had registered the violence and the best result would be an instant divorce.

"But I am not ready yet. I cannot let go. Like you, I have been hanging onto a dead relationship. There will come a time... Until then, my ring stays on my finger."

She looked across at Cameron and said, "Are we not both rather stubborn?"

Cameron's voice was soothing in his reply, "A stubbornness born of mis-attached love. There are worse things in the world."

Cameron looked up and held her gaze for a long time before looking again at the stunning horizon. Melody joined him gazing out at the fading sun. Enjoying the beauty of the moment together, a quiet contentment descended between them.

9

Wisdom

Elaine watched Cameron come out of his office and walk across the school yard. He always had a mild look of sadness about him but this time he looked puzzled, as if he could not think something through. His head looked down as he moved, lost in his own thoughts.

Most of the children were on a break, so the schoolyard was full of noisy students chatting and playing. Something added to the cacophony and Elaine saw Cameron snap his head to the corner of the yard as a child's scream pierced the air. The sound had a knife edge of pain to it that was different from the normal play noises and he ran to the origins of the scream, his thoughts abandoned.

In the far corner of the playground to Elaine's left, a boy about ten years old was lying with his back on the ground under a tree. He had fallen out of the tree. As Cameron approached he saw that under the boy's lower back there was a branch; it would have been very painful to land on that.

Several children had gathered round and Elaine saw that more teachers were coming across. Cameron told one of them to call an ambulance as the boy could not move his legs. Elaine felt a moment of fear deep in her belly. What would happen to the boy, was he badly hurt?

The ambulance arrived from the road to Elaine's right. The teachers cleared the way so it could drive straight across the schoolyard to where the boy was lying. They quickly managed to calm him, put him on a stretcher and drove off, one of the teachers going with them.

Elaine turned again to look at Cameron. The other adults had dispersed but he remained standing, looking to where the ambulance had disappeared. The other children had resumed playing, a group of girls chasing each other just next to Cameron. One of them noticed Elaine watching and came over and spoke to her. "His bones will knit back together without difficulty. He will be back next week, trying to play football with crutches. That'll be fun to watch, you'll see." She touched Elaine's arm and smiled, then went back to playing.

A small boy, probably six years old, approached Cameron. He stopped about a meter away before approaching again and tugging at the older man's sleeve. "Hey, hey you. Stop worrying. You're lookin' in the wrong place. They won't help you here. You have to look elsewhere. But you can't see anymore for worrying."

Elaine stepped nearer and listened in. This was interesting; she had never heard a young boy speak like that to a grown-up before.

Cameron was taken aback, "What do you mean?"

One of the girls, older than the others, stopped whirling around and joined in, "It's obvious isn't it? If you won't get the energy machine accepted here, then you will have to get it done elsewhere."

Cameron was still recovering from his shock. Elaine was puzzled. Cameron normally seemed to be so calm and self-assured. He reminded her of Mole. It was odd to see him disoriented. She walked up to him and touched his arm, "I think they are trying to tell you something. Doesn't this happen all the time here?"

The girl laughed lightly, seeming more mature than her eleven years, "Cameron rarely needs any advice from us, he's usually in tune with himself. But since his wife died he has been troubled and now he worries. He wants to be sure what happens but you can't and he's forgotten that."

Another teacher, Jack, came over. Cameron explained what they were talking about, the advice from the boy to take the patenting of the V-Gen abroad.

"I wondered why the children were hard to get back in class," said Jack. "You know Cameron, it is a good idea. The patent here could be pending for years, they are doing more than just dragging their feet. If we let the schools in the US push it through, there we could move it forward very quickly."

Elaine joined in, "Why don't you let my friend Mole help? He's very good with bureaucracy."

Jack and Cameron took no notice of the suggestion. The little boy tugged again at Cameron's shirt, "You're ignoring your dreams as well. You have to follow your dreams. They are going to get stronger. Don't wait too long."

Jack looked across at Cameron, "What are your dreams doing?"

"They are telling me to go on a long journey," answered Cameron.

"On your bicycle," shouted a little girl as she danced around and around with her friends.

Jack's eyes widened as he tried to take this all in. "So what are you going to do now?"

"I don't know," said Cameron. The idea of cycling again had hit him like a hurricane and he was in shock. Cycling? He had not been on his bike since the accident. He had lived through enough sweaty nights with nightmares of bicycles and broken bodies to know that going on a bicycle tour would be the biggest challenge of his life.

"Well at least we can start looking at this American idea before you check out whether your bicycle tires are pumped up," put in Jack. He realized what Cameron's problem was and grinned from ear to ear. If the guy was dreaming about cycling then this was one fear he was going to have to tackle sooner or later. Knowing Cameron, it might be sooner.

Cameron looked back at him and asked, "Do you know anyone in the schools over there?"

"Don't forget the Kiwis," shouted one boy. "All that steppin' on you, they know how to keep themselves clear. You've lost touch with them, but not them with you. They're more of a help than all your foolishness. Look to New Zealand."

Cameron walked away, shaking his head. He had no idea what it all meant, but he did know it was best to heed every word. The little ones tended to be very good at prediction.

10

The Cave

Elaine, Melody and Cameron waited for the other tourists to continue the tour through to the next cave. Cameron nodded to the tourist guide who checked that no one else was left behind as he moved the rest of the visitors deeper into the earth. They were alone.

"Now, take your time, just get a sense of the atmosphere of this place," said Cameron. They were standing in the centre of the cave, which was dimly lit by electric lights just above head height. The darkness gathering above their heads obscured the ceiling fifteen meters above them. The entrance to the cave was through a narrow tunnel, one and a half meters high, requiring most people to bend down in order to enter. Now they were in the middle of a large oblong cave, roughly forty-five meters long and twenty-five meters wide. The sides of the cave sloped into the centre, giving a limited amount of flat space for the tourists. The air was cool and damp, a tinkling of running water always present. Elaine and Melody strolled around, going into different corners and looking at the back of the cave, trying to take a peek at the ledge that was about three meters off the floor on one side.

Once they were finished, Cameron took them outside. They ducked their heads to go through the low passageway that led back to the entrance. As they walked along they noticed the point at which the air became warmer. The switch from cool cave air to the outside conditions was abrupt. They were still inside the hill, but with daylight flooding through from the large gap at the front of this cave, it no longer felt so claustrophobic. At one side of the wide mouth of the entrance, a group of tourists were being taken through a demonstration of the ancient art of rope making. They passed by the tourists and came out into the open air, the late summer sun almost blinding them after the darkness inside. The fenced path descended gently from the entrance, with the cliff faces on each side widening out until they were back walking in the open air. On reaching the road they turned left and headed for the hills just in front of them. After a mile the road started to become steep and narrow, but they continued on, walking on the footpath next to the road. They turned right at the top of the steep hill and came to where the road just ended, with a few parking spaces and a picnic bench and table. Melody and Cameron laid out a cloth and some simple food from their rucksacks, bread, cheese, pickled onions and cucumbers, and they all sat down.

From here they could see the whole of the panorama around them. The land was separated into fields of coarse grass by stone walls. Most of the fields were full of sheep. A few strays were eating the grass along the roadside, having found the way through where the stone walls had collapsed and fallen into disrepair. To the right they could see the town of Castleton and the wooded area surrounding the cave they had just explored. Behind them was the great Mam Tor hill.

"So why did you bring me here?" asked Elaine.

Melody and Cameron looked at each other and laughed, the sound surprising Elaine, her face creasing up in a frown.

"It's OK," said Melody. "It's just you were so direct, it was unexpected."

"We brought you out today because the cave is a special place. Let's have a little history lesson. This will be really fascinating and unlike any history you have had before.

"Throughout the ages there have always been different religions. Thousands of years ago, the Celts were the main folk here and their religious leaders were the Druids. We know now about many of the ceremonies the Druids kept, worshiping a God in their holy places in nature, in sacred groves of trees, often oaks."

"That's why so many old places are called Seven Oaks?" asked Elaine.

"Yes," replied Cameron. "But as well as the public ceremonies they also had hidden rituals that they performed away from the open gaze. Most people did not even know these rites existed. They were special ceremonies of initiation performed by the priests. These were to be found in nearly all religions and were called the Mysteries. Their very existence was kept secret and the rites performed were considered sacred."

Elaine jumped in, "Why were they kept secret?" she asked.

"Patience, I will come to that," answered Cameron. "The cave we just came out of has a wide open mouth where the rope making was demonstrated. If you go further in, you have to duck down to get through a narrow passage before entering into the central chamber. That passage is artificial. Years ago the only way into that chamber was to swim through an underground stream that has now mostly dried up. Centuries ago the Druids performed their initiation ceremonies there. The candidate for initiation was brought into the outer cave and told to go into the stream and swim. He was not told anything else and did not know that there was anything on the other side. If he swam carefully he would come out into the cave."

"And if he wasn't careful," joined in Melody, "he would either swim back out again or drown."

"It was a test of trust and courage. If he reached the chamber then the initiation rite was performed and he was accepted into the inner circle," continued Cameron. "There he learned the mystery secrets known to that circle."

Melody continued, "So the cave was a place where secret holy rites were performed. All across the world secret knowledge was held by small enclosed groups who had initiation rites to ensure that those people who gained access to the knowledge had the moral fiber to ensure that the information was not misused."

"Because knowledge was power," said Cameron. "With some of this you could rule whole kingdoms. The people who gained access to this knowledge should be those who would use it for the good of their community and not for their own personal power. The Mystery centers, as they were called, were so set up that those who were not in control of their own ego impulses were never invited to initiation, or they failed the final initiation tests."

"And so it continued through hundreds of years," said Melody, "until the nineteenth century.

Then, for the first time, some of that knowledge became available to all. This started off as a trickle but continued all through the twentieth century until it was pouring out into the public realm."

"Was there not still a danger that the knowledge could be misused?" asked Elaine.

"Yes there was," replied Melody. "However, it was obvious that we were now moving toward our Era, the Age of the Individual, when each human has reached a level of development where they can make their own decisions about what to do with their lives, with their own refined sense of morality to guide them, and no longer need to be controlled by the rules of rigid societies to ensure their standards of thought and behavior."

"So, our school is built around just one of those pieces of knowledge," continued Cameron, "and that piece of knowledge is how to structure your thinking."

"Although we bring in many more things as well," added Melody.

Elaine giggled, "Do you always do this - first one, then the other, first Cameron, then Melody? You should do your own Net show, "Cam and Mel's Laugh Hour', you'd be a sure-fire hit."

Melody and Cameron looked surprised. They had not realized what they were doing. They turned to each other and laughed, Melody going notably red in the face.

Cameron continued, "Well, last time we met we began to tell you how it works. How you can layer the thought structures so they fall into four layers, from earth, plant and animal to human, which then can be thought of as physical, life, mind and then spirit levels. Did you have any more thoughts about that?"

"I was thinking about how it works out in the lessons. Now you have pointed it out it seems clear that some lessons are structured into four layers. Other lessons appear to be but then they continue past the fourth levels and I don't understand what's happening anymore. It's almost as if they go off on a different subject but there again they are not, it's still the same lesson, just done differently. So I knew there was something more to it than what you explained before. But I was also wondering how you use it."

"Well, I can give you an example of what happens in our meetings," said Cameron. "We consider each theme like this. First we have a basic description of what the theme is. That is the basic physical layer. Then we go through the history of the subject, how did it occur. That is the life layer. Only then do we discuss it, the discussion being the mind layer. Finally we reach a conclusion about the subject, this is then the spirit layer."

"I've never attended such meetings. How does that differ from how others do it?" asked Elaine.

"First, we are very conscious about the four layers," answered Cameron. "Keeping them separate aids clarity. You introduce a topic. Then, by going through the history of how something came about you get a much better understanding of the situation. This reduces a lot of unnecessary blah, blah, blah in the next layer, the mind layer. There we discuss the subject, getting different opinions. We are also very much aware of the fact that after discussing an item we then have a last layer, which is the decision making layer. This makes us all more conscious about decisions and how they affect what we do. We sometimes find people who are very good at discussing all evening but who then are unable to make a final decision."

"What do you do when you cannot reach a decision?" asked Elaine between bites of her sandwich.

"As far as the thinking structure is concerned, that's not a problem. There's a whole range of thought structures that can be used as well as the four level structure that we told you about last time. That's what some of your teachers are doing."

Cameron continued to tell her more about thought structure. How the structuring of the thinking was not just about going through four layers. You could also take it further, continuing back down the layers, how a transformation of the subject was built into the structure.

"That gets complicated," said Elaine. "Now I understand why I couldn't follow the lesson structure anymore. But this transformation business makes sense. The lessons do then go off in a different direction but it is still the same thing that is being taught. Wow, that's really something! I would find it dead boring to do that all the time, don't you think?"

"Sometimes it seems rigid and confining, like being put into a mental straight jacket," replied Cameron. "Some who learn it and start using it stop doing so after a few years. But then they find using their heads in the usual way leaves them with an odd feeling, a vague sense of being cold and isolated. After a while we have grown to think of this type of thinking as Natural Thinking.

"There's a strange effect of the type of thinking we use here. It progressively opens people's hearts, giving them a greater capacity for empathy. It seems almost a contradiction sometimes, that what you do with your head affects your heart. After working this way for a while you open up, and become more aware and appreciative of those around you and less interested in yourself. You develop a stronger capability of Love. The method affects your ability to be intuitive, to such an extent that an Intuition, instead of being a momentary, Eureka phenomenon, becomes a flow of consciousness that can last for minutes, if not hours. That's why it's appropriate that this method is sometimes called Heart-Thinking. Those who use it are Heart People. There are many groups of Heart People, not just those involved in Heart-Thinking. In fact, you could say that most of the people who live outside the cities are Heart People. So here we have Heart People, using Natural Thinking to develop their Heart-Thinking."

Elaine remained silent, mulling things over. All at once the birds twittered overhead and the sounds of the sheep moving around the field seemed louder.

"But why...' Elaine started. "But why do you have teachers like, well, you know, like Joel? He's just a bastard!"

Melody remained silent. It was Cameron who replied, "There are largely two streams of people who are interested in this type of learning. The first are the Creatives, artistic people. They are not so fascinated by logical things but this construction is something they can work with. The Creatives can then use Heart-Thinking as a way of helping them communicate with the world. The second is the more logical people. They are usually quite stuck in their heads. They catch on to the logic of using Heart-Thinking very quickly. It helps them to make the bridge and understand creative people more. It also has the effect of softening them up, making them easy-going and rounded.

"Here at the school we need both. We need the Creatives who can relate to so many of the students here. We also need the great thinkers who can understand the intricacies of the Heart-Thinking logic. Joel is one of the great thinkers here.

"What we find important though is that the two different types of personality learn to live and work with each other. For centuries artists and scientists have lived side by side but never learnt to understand or get on with each other. This method gets over that problem. Later on in the school, we get students to work with each other in pairs, a creative and logic person together. For example, they learn how to design their own meditations. The creative person is very good at finding the original words and text. The logic person can then take the words and form them into a heart-thinking structure. The other way round is difficult - the logical person would find it hard to find their own initial words and the creative might find it impossible to put them into a logical structure. Together, using the best of their individual talents, the two types of personality can learn to build something better than either could do on their own. It's true team work."

There was silence while Elaine picked at her food, thinking things over. "I thought I was going to learn to see Angels and Fairies and other stuff. What's the good of all this thinking to me?" she asked.

"The problems of the world can only be solved when people develop their own consciousness, their own way of thinking and understanding who they are and what they do in the world," replied Cameron. "Once human beings grasp that their awareness is the main thing that they develop through their lives on earth, then the difficulties here in the world will be much easier to solve. For the only thing that you can alter is your own thinking, and through that you affect everything around you.

"Changing how people think about the world is the key to the salvation of humanity on the earth. That's what the structural thinking gives you in your life and through you, affects the rest of the world."

Melody added, "Everyone in the Western world is taught how to think. This is just a new way of doing it. But with this you can get very structured in your thinking and still be intuitive. The old way hindered intuitions. This way encourages it, that's the beauty of this technique. And later on, if you go into other sorts of practices, you'll find you can do that and Heart-Thinking at the same time. One method does not prevent you from seeking another path in any way. Far from it."

Elaine looked down at the ground and waited only a second before coming forth with her next question, "Some of the other kids were talking about Domes. What are they? Why are they necessary?"

"Well, we told you last time about Melody's parents and how they were affected by the Branching. This event happened across the earth in a couple of days. We don't know for sure, but we reckon about half of the people were aware of a change going on, or were asked what their choice in life was, as the example of Melody's father illustrates. For the other half of humanity, it passed them by, just another day.

"For those connected with the good, they became more aware of their conscious surroundings."

"Their what?" asked Elaine.

"Thoughts," said Cameron.

"And emotions," added Melody.

"It's like this," said Cameron. "Imagine your thoughts are like little white, fluffy clouds, some the size of table tennis balls, others as big as your bedroom. Now, when you think a thought, you create one of these fluffy clouds. If it is a light, happy thought, it is a light, fluffy cloud. If it is a dark, brooding thought then it is a dark ugly looking cloud."

"These thoughts can hang around your body," continued Melody. "Or if you are thinking about a particular person, then those thoughts go to that person and hang around them. So what you think has an immediate effect on the world around you. If you think about another person, then that thought has an immediate effect on that other person."

Cameron continued, "After the Branching, some people became aware of these thoughts all around them. We also think that whatever happened in the Branching caused the thoughts and emotions of everyone to be much stronger, to have an almost physical effect on the world. The most sensitive could connect to a person next to them and understand every thought the other was thinking. Others were not so sensitive and could only tell when someone was directly thinking about them. Most could get a rough impression for what was happening in a room or a place. Over time, living in the cities became strenuous for these people. Cities are full of all sorts of thoughts, mostly pretty egoistical and emotional stuff. This is often flying around or settling in the places in which it was created. It feels like you are moving through a thick glop of consciousness."

Melody went on, "The sensitive people could no longer survive in the cities so they moved out to the country, full of fresh air and nature, which was refreshing and inspiring. This happened over a few years, people often leaving in small groups."

"And this is what we call the Exodus from the Cities," said Cameron. "However, for some, that still did not help. If the wind blew from the wrong direction then this conscious glop would be blown out of the city with it. Imagine, you're sitting there happily tidying your garden, it's a nice day, the sun is shining, then suddenly this thought-glop descends on you. This grew to be highly irritating. So someone came up with the great idea of putting Domes around the cities."

"It's a simple idea," said Melody. "The Dome is an invisible energy screen which surrounds a city and stops the conscious glop getting outside. It stops low grade emotions and negative thoughts, nothing else."

"What d'you mean, it bounces the thoughts back into the people in the city to make their lives extra miserable?" asked Elaine.

"No," replied Cameron, "that would generate a steamed up atmosphere in there. A city Dome absorbs the thoughts that hit its surface. The thought is absorbed, neither going outside the Dome, nor being reflected back in. In this way the outside world is protected from the conscious pollution from the cities."

"But I lived all my life in London and never saw or heard such a thing," exclaimed Elaine.

"You cannot see them," said Melody. "And if you do not know they are there, it is hard to imagine. Perhaps some would notice that the atmosphere in the countryside seems clearer and refreshing, but they would maybe put that down to the fresh air."

"So you see why we put so much emphasis on thinking in our school. It directly affects your whole environment and life."

"But that's extraordinary," said Elaine. She peered off looking at some hikers climbing a nearby hill, lost in thought. After quite a while she came back to herself.

"So which class do we learn to see Angels in then?" she asked.

The others just laughed, disturbing the sheep with their noise.

11

The Museum

Cameron walked up the steps and into the foyer of the stone building, going through the security checks along with all the other tourists streaming in. The recent terrorism alerts did not seem to have dampened the enthusiasm for visiting London, nor the British Museum. Security alerts in London were as regular as chicken pox in Kindergarten; people were just used to it and took it in their stride.

He moved past the entrance, and into the huge circular hall. Built of white stone, it was an airy central room, giving an impression of light and space. He asked at the information desk where to go and was directed into the first exhibit room off the central chamber, opposite the entrance.

There, in a corner, he found the crystal skull. It was displayed in a transparent case standing on its own, on a little white stand. You could look but you could not touch. He read the information displayed about the crystal skull. It had been found in the nineteenth century. Under close examination it had been discovered that the crystal had regular, minute cuts in it, which seemed to be evidence that it had been made mechanically. This seemed to disprove the idea that it had originated from an ancient civilization. Instead, it was suggested that the crystal had been manufactured sometime in the early nineteenth century. At least, that was what the display said. Cameron wanted to see for himself.

He stared at it for a long time. Although the skull was untouchable inside its display, it was well lit by bright white lamps on the ceiling. The crystal seemed to glow in the light and he was fascinated.

Was this what he had been dreaming about? The skull looked harmless enough in its case. He wandered around so he could see it from all sides. He thought the teeth looked odd as they were all joined up rather than separate pieces. It was the only part of the skull that disturbed him. For the rest of it was a life-size replica of a human skull, the beauty of the underlying stone highlighted by the lighting.

No one else seemed interested in the skull, so he stayed there. He stood still, and entered into a meditative state watching it. He focused on the skull, opening his mind to it.

"Can I help you?" asked a female voice beside him. He had not heard anyone approach, and was startled at the nearby voice. He took a step to one side, away from the sound of the voice, missed his footing and ended up stepping wildly in a different direction, trying to regain his balance, and bumping into the nearby wall.

Facing him was a woman of medium height, conservatively dressed, with straight brown hair surrounding a pleasant face. "Do you always have that effect on men or is it just me?" asked Cameron.

The woman's face split into a large smile, "My name is Rebecca Smeed. I'm a researcher here. The security guards noticed you were spending a long time looking at the crystal. The skull sometimes attracts fanatics who have been known to try and break into the cabinet and steal it. I saw you on the security monitors and decided to come up and take a look. You don't appear too much like a fanatic."

"Perhaps if I ruffled my hair and put on a wild eyed look, I might fit the bill better," Cameron said. A grin lit up his face to let her know he was joking.

She laughed gently, "Is it possible we have met before?"

Cameron hesitated, "My picture is sometimes to be found in obscure Net Magazines. My name is Cameron Trevelyn. I administer a Heart Voyance School in Derbyshire."

Her face dropped, and the smile vanished, to be replaced by one raised eyebrow. "I have never met anyone like you before." She hesitated before continuing. "Perhaps you would care for a coffee?"

They retired to the cafeteria area, and sat down at a small round table in the open plan eating area. There were about twenty tables altogether in the cafeteria, most of them empty, with few visitors needing refreshments so early. Rebecca told him what she knew about crystal skulls and he asked her various pointed questions about their origins. Other than the official opinion that they were not antique but were probably made by craftsmen at the beginning of the nineteenth century, he learnt nothing new.

"So, enough of fake antiques," said Rebecca. "I have never met anyone from a Heart Voyance School. Tell me, what made you join?"

Cameron told her about his early days involved in science research. How he had realized when working on his PhD that the greatest discoveries were made by very intuitive people, who were out of the ordinary in their own field and who took quite a different approach to their peers. When he tried to find out how intuition worked and whether you could train it like any other capacity of the mind, he found various different groups which claimed they could do so. The Heart Voyance School attracted him the most as it was based on logic. This appealed to him on the one hand because he had already received and enjoyed a structured education, and on the other because it seemed to him the most plausible approach to Intuition.

"So, I started learning about how it worked and did a basic two year course," Cameron told her. "After that it seemed a natural progression to become a teacher at one of the schools. When my wife died I lost interest in teaching, and moved to the position of school administrator which I am now in. I do quite a bit of coordination with the other schools in the country, and some abroad, and am enjoying what I do."

Cameron was beginning to relax, and as he did so, he noticed his heart energy unfolding. He decided to give it some assistance and beamed it at Rebecca. He was silent for a while concentrating on sending this beam of pure love to the person opposite him.

"It just seems quite sad really," she said, crossing her legs to one side and brushing some dust off her jacket, her eyes looking over at the entrance door.

"Why?" asked Cameron, his voice higher pitched, the beginnings of a frown appearing on his forehead.

"You are clearly such a highly educated, intelligent man. It seems such a complete loss to see you fritter away your time on this worthless nonsense. No one can change their intuition, there is no such thing anyway. It's just a spark of particular neurons.

You are wasting your time and energy when society needs people of your caliber to be making a proper contribution."

Cameron was so surprised that words first failed him. Hadn't the connection between energy and consciousness been fully established and accepted? Not in this world obviously. This was like being dropped into twentieth century dead thinking. Was this what Sleepers thought? Perhaps it was a fitting idea to find in a museum. He began talking slowly. "You know to get into London from the North, I had to take the train and go through two full body scanners. They are sophisticated machines that can detect if a person has been working with firearms within the past week."

"That's what I mean," interrupted Rebecca. "You could be employed making machines such as that."

"London has become a fortress. The people inside have barricaded themselves in, scared of so-called terrorists. Things have been getting worse as this century progresses. More and more energy and effort have been put into building highly sophisticated but ultimately useless machines, such as the firearm scanners. Why are they useless? Because they fail to tackle the one big problem we have: how do we learn to live together in peace and harmony. In order to do that we need two things: we need new ideas, and we also need to learn how to develop mutual empathy. To put it simply, we need creativity and love. Love to bring us together, creativity to help us get out of this situation. We have had over four hundred years of relying on our intellect, and without mankind developing further beyond its wits, it's going to drive us further into the abyss."

Rebecca stood up, "I was wrong about you," she said. "You really are a fanatic. Goodbye, Mr. Trevelyn." She strode out of the cafeteria.

It had been a long time since he had been to the city, and this intellectual view on life was something he had not heard in a while. It shocked him to find that such cold, destructive opinions were distributed without reflection. It was heartless.

The conversation had been progressing well; he had been making a human connection to Rebecca. The abrupt departure had been unexpected, if not shocking. He looked back on the flow of the exchange - when had it altered? The first meeting at the skull was no problem, otherwise they would not have ended up in the cafeteria. So when had it shifted?

The answer dawned on him. Her body language had changed when he had started deliberately sending heart energy to her. She had instinctively looked away, the wave of love not something she wished to accept. This wasn't the reaction he would have had back home. Could she not receive it? Were people so far-gone in the Dome that they could not open their hearts at all?

Cameron got up, shaken. It had been an unsuccessful day. He headed for the door, quickly moving out to get into the fresh air. He went down the small streets, trying to stay away from the crowds at Tottenham Court Road until the last minute.

He emerged onto a busy street. There was a squash of men and women on the pavement trying to avoid a small plump man who was shouting incoherently at people, his anger clear from his tone and his clenched fists. He was carrying a billboard and when the crowds cleared, Cameron could see what was written on it, "Sinners repent, Save Yourself from Hell." His angry tone was a perfect addition to the unpleasant atmosphere of the Dome. Cameron wondered if he had ever heard of a God of Love?

On an impulse Cameron changed his direction and took the underground to Charing Cross station, returning to daylight in Trafalgar Square. He had not yet decided whether to head for the river or Green Park, when a man caught his eye, standing on the pavement next to a lamppost on the other side of the square. He had his left arm extended straight up. It looked as if he was propping up the lamppost unless you examined further and saw that the fingers of his left hand made a strange figure. The forefinger and the middle finger were pointing straight up, with the thumb also pointing upwards, placed between them. The ring finger and small finger were curled down.

The thumb and two fingers pointing up in a three. This was the sign for distress.

On seeing him Cameron immediately changed course. Weaving through the tourists, he hopped across the square and approached the stranger. "Greetings, you look a bit stuck there! First time in a Dome?"

The man turned to look at him. He had black straight hair and piercing blue eyes in an angular face. Tall and thin, he was dressed in an expensive brown raincoat, dark trousers and leather shoes peeking out underneath. He lowered his hand and faced Cameron. "Tom. Where are you from?"

"Cameron. The Heart Voyance School in Castleton, and you?"

"Kings Lynn farming community." Cameron nodded. He had heard of the Kings Lynn farming community. They managed to span being a community for mentally handicapped as well as doing the highest of the new agricultural research, the scientists themselves often moving straight from the labs to the resident's houses to help with the evening meal and other duties. He found it strange that one of them would be caught here.

"You need help?"

"I can't stop thinking about her." Tom looked pained, almost ashamed to admit it.

Cameron took in what he was seeing. It was always possible for a heart person to become lost in a Dome, which was why the distress sign had been invented. You just went out to the street and stuck your hand in the air with the three fingers extended. The Sleepers never noticed, but if any Heart People were about they stopped what they were doing and went to help.

This case with Tom was already clear to Cameron. If he was showing signs of shame, then his basic sense of morality was intact. The problem was coming from outside. "She's swamping you. We'll have to bubble up."

"If you bubble up, I won't be able to feel her anymore." His voice was cracked and Cameron felt sorry for him. It was one thing for the Sleepers to lose themselves in infatuation, but it was quite another for a heart person. If you could not clear it away, you would be lost in this emotion of the other and would never leave the Dome. You would remember the other world and another simpler way of life and you would long for what you had lost. For some, unable to reconcile the memories of a golden age with the present lifestyle, the speed of self-destruction was supersonic.

A difficult situation to get out of. Not thinking about the woman would never work. The trick was to get them to think of something else. He needed to concentrate on something else until he got out of here, and the Dome worked in his favor. It was an age-old technique - focus on the good things, rather than focusing on denying the bad things. Cameron was direct rather than polite. "You have lost your stability. If I don't bubble up you will become lost in here. Is this how you want to live? You choose now - should I help you or not?"

Tom looked at him, his eyes moist and nodded his head. Cameron started the bubble up process. It was quite simple. You put the other person in an egg shaped energy field of white energy. Cameron started it off, picturing the energy field around Tom, starting from about fifty centimeters below his feet, forming this round shape surrounding him, finishing off with the top of the egg, or bubble, fifty centimeters above the person's head. The basic shape was completed in a few minutes, then he imagined it filled with white light.

"You're done. Go home and don't come back into a Dome for the next six months."

"But I need to…"

"You need to go and save your soul. You have lost your balance here and you won't regain it so long as you are in the Dome. Go home, where you are loved, not lusted after."

"I am not sure if I can make it."

"No problem. Just keep this mantra repeating in your mind. Say: "omnipotent reigneth". That will keep you on track until you are outside the Dome."

Tom gave a short sad smile. "Thank you," he said, putting one hand out to squeeze Cameron's upper arm before turning around. He took one step but then turned round a puzzled look on his face. "Omnipotent reigneth? That's part of the Hallelujah chorus isn't it?" Cameron just nodded. Tom said, "That means I'm going to have the Hallelujah chorus rattling around my head the whole journey home. God, I don't believe it, I don't even like that tune!' He laughed and walked away.

Cameron headed for the Tube station, the first step in the long journey home. Some days everything felt difficult. He had lost the knack of working with Sleepers. He had helped Tom, though.

12

School Meeting

Cameron stood in a corner of the room looking out at the surrounding hillside. He had felt as if his life was emerging out of the darkness, heading back towards pleasant peacefulness. Everything had seemed to be running smoothly. His intuition had returned, he was working with pupils again. The research institute had found a way of producing almost unlimited energy, solving the worst crisis in the world. The only thing you needed to run the V-Gen generators was water.

Now all that had changed. The government seemed to want to swallow the V-Gen patenting in red tape, doing everything from microscopically examining the phrasing to employing a team of scientists to generate reams of paperwork questioning the safety of the machines.

The school system itself was under attack. This was a response to the V-Gen generator. Shut the school down and the energy machine dies with it. So, how to secure the school was the topic at hand. The other teachers had been informed and would be gathering now. He was used to leading them, but he had no answers and wondered how to proceed. If they did not manage to change this new government policy, it would be the death of the school.

The meeting room filled up until there were ten of them. Some, like Daniel Price, were silent, brooding, their thoughtfulness not producing any useful results. Others were voracious with indignant anger. Jack came over and wanted to talk to him about something the children had said, but Cameron asked him to approach him afterwards, as he did not want a distraction now. The rest were lively. How dare the government do this! It was going to be an eventful discussion.

At last, Cathy and Joel arrived, talking vigorously as they came in.

Cameron opened up the meeting, introducing their one topic. Their normal discipline disappeared with the wind. A rabble chorus they became, all speaking at the same time, no one listening to the next participant. Cameron remained quiet. He waited. They needed to get rid of enough emotion so that they could become calmer and regain their inner stillness. This was going to take some time. He wondered whether it was even going to be possible. After all, this was something threatening their very way of life, not just their jobs.

His attention was abruptly brought back to the meeting. Someone was asking him his opinion. Now was the time to turn the meeting around.

"Let's look at this from the basics," Cameron said. "We have a new cabinet who, after spending two years looking at the educational situation, have decided that not only will they set the curriculum for all schools, they will also provide the teaching materials for the lessons. There can be no opt-out for private schools, and everyone must use the same lesson plan.

"For us, this is a major change. Previously, if any government required private schools to teach certain subjects, we could always take the subject and teach it in our own philosophy. Now we will be forbidden to do so. It's a really difficult situation and there seems no obvious way forward. That's why we are so worked up. Have we forgotten which way we have for dealing with such situations? Has fear got to us or are we asleep?

"Let us sit quietly now and see what ideas come, in our usual fashion."

They went into the routine, stopping talking and settling down as best as they could. Quickly the room went quiet, although the atmosphere was still tense.

They all stayed silent for a long while. One by one they opened their eyes, staring at the walls or making small notes until they were all back from their ponderings.

This time was different. Randomly they started to give their comments, "I got nothing."

"Me neither."

"I am just too worked up."

"Like looking at a brick wall, nothing came."

One of the teachers, Lia, moved forward in her chair. She opened her mouth but did not start talking, she just coughed.

"Go on, Lia," said Cameron.

"I got something, but I don't know what it means." She stopped short.

"Do you want to tell us?" asked Cameron.

"OK, as you ask. I asked the question, 'how can we save our school?' I did get something, but I don't understand. As an answer, I just got a picture of you, Cameron, riding a bicycle. That was it."

Cameron's jaw dropped, comically, leaving his mouth wide open like a fish.

"I got the same thing," said Cathy. "Just Cameron riding a bicycle. Normally the meaning of what we see is obvious. I didn't get this one, but *you* understand it. That's written all over your face. Tell us what it means, Cameron."

Slowly, Cameron started telling them about his dreams, going in search of the crystal skull, what he had found out about them from Melody and what the children had said in the playground about riding on his bicycle.

"Does that mean you are proposing to just get on your bike and ride off into the wild to, well, God only knows where?" said Joel. "You're not serious?"

The others looked from Cameron to Joel and back again.

"I think he should go," said Lia.

Joel made a false snigger. "You have got to be joking. Go where? Cycle across the ocean to New York like a modern day savior? Come off it. Not only is Cameron our best public representative, he is also the one with the most direct contacts to the other school systems. If anyone can coordinate a solid framework of defense against this proposal from the government, then it's him.

"Look what it means if we lose this fight. If we are forced to use the government's materials in our lessons then we cannot put in the intuitive thinking structure. The whole purpose behind what we are doing is lost. We might as well pack in our jobs and go and work in the city."

Uproar greeted this. Everyone started to talk at once, backwards and forwards across the table. Their usual composure was lost again and it looked like it was gone for good this time. Cameron could smell an underlying sense of fear in the room, something which he now realized was absent from their usual meetings. He understood well enough though, if they could not find a way through this issue then they would have to close the school.

He let the discussion go on for a while but there was no settling down. Things were beginning to get heated when he decided to intervene.

"Talking on like this is getting us nowhere," said Cameron. "Let's calm down and talk one by one."

"What's there to talk about?" said Joel. "There is only one thing for you to do. Get the Federation of Heart Voyance Schools together and start a campaign of protest, both legal and political. Let's muster every friend and ex-pupil we ever had and get them to fight this."

Several heads started nodding in approval.

Cathy looked up, first at Joel and then at Cameron before speaking. "We are a Heart Voyance School, that is what we teach. That is also what we live by. I don't know where this will go or how it will work, but I do know that in times of trouble, if we do not live by what we teach, then we are lost. There is only one course of action for me. I think Cameron should get on his bike and go search for the crystal skull."

Joel's response was immediate, his voice so loud it was verging on shouting, "Are you in your right mind? How do we know the pictures you got were real? Aren't there enough cases in history of leaders creating catastrophes because God told them so?" He slammed his fist down on the table. "Are you going to throw away everything we have achieved here? For what? Cameron gets on his bike and goes on a tour through the wilds in search of an ancient legend? What's he going to do, dig up a piece of crystal by an old stream and say hey Abracadabra, Heart Voyance Schools are OK again?" Joel turned to Cameron, "Tell her she's nuts."

"Is she?" asked Cameron.

Joel looked stunned, "You don't mean to say you believe this nonsense? This is lunacy. I am not staying here to listen to you all destroy this school."

Joel stormed out the room, leaving a quaking silence behind him.

"So what do you intend to do Cameron?" asked Cathy, quietly.

"I don't know. I just don't know. I am so unclear, like I've never been before," replied Cameron.

"Well, I know what I'm going to do," said Jack, as he made his way to the door. "I'm off. To Christchurch, New Zealand, as no one is asking."

Cathy gave Jack a puzzled look and then turned to Cameron, before getting up, and picking up her pieces of paper to take with her. "One thing is sure, the decision as to whether you go is not for us to make." She stared at him. "It's yours alone to decide, Cameron." As she walked out of the room, the others began to follow. Eventually Cameron was left alone, still sitting, his head in his hands.

He got up and headed for the door. He hit the wall switch that would seal the room as soon as everyone had left.

Cameron started walking towards the town and almost stumbled in the dark. He did not see Elaine standing to one side observing him. Once he walked past her in the dark, her face took on a sorrowful grimace and she headed back towards her house.

Cameron wanted to head up into the hills, to let the air cool his face and blow away his troubled thoughts. His physical energy had deserted him. He wandered the back streets for a while, then sat down on a bench in a small public garden, just off the main street of town.

His feet would not remain still though, and he had to keep changing position. His mind wandered all over the place, almost trying to avoid the question at hand. He glanced over to the street. The occasional passers-by could be seen over the top of the hedge at the edge of the garden.

The next passer-by seemed familiar, even in silhouette from the street lamps. He softly called her name, "Melody." She turned in his direction and peered into the darkness of the small park. He stood up, and after taking a few paces towards her, she recognized him and moved into the garden.

"What's wrong?" she asked, seeing the furrows on his forehead. They took their seats on the bench and he started to explain. When he came to the end of his tale she asked him, "What do you want to do?"

He looked into the dark at the far side of the garden. "I just don't know. Whenever I have followed my intuition in the past I have usually known what the outcome would be or that the consequences were not so important. Now it seems as if the whole school system depends on what decision I make. Joel is right, I can bring all the independent schools together for a united campaign. And I haven't a clue what would happen if I went away. My head tells me I should stay and my heart tells me to go."

His turmoil drew her towards him. She moved closer along the bench, stretched out her arm and squeezed his shoulder. Cameron moved his head round towards her. He picked up her outstretched hand and rubbed it against his cheek. His staring eyes looked straight at hers and their glance held for a long time. He moved his other hand towards her cheek, caressing it before moving towards her. They kissed gently for a long time.

Cameron pulled back and stared at her. He stood up, nearly losing his footing and awkwardly stepping to one side, all the time looking at her. "I…" he began to say.

Melody came to his rescue. "I am a married woman and you have decisions to make. When you are ready, then we will see." She stood up and without further comment, walked out of the garden, leaving him alone in the shadows.

13

The Storm

Cameron meandered his way up the hillside, too lost in his thoughts to cut a straight line. The darkened clouds formed a low ceiling, with the air below clear, so he could see how the storm was developing above the Moors.

He wandered up to a large cherry tree perched on the ridge, one of his favorite places to rest. The beautiful view of the green valley below was cast in darkness. He had come here looking for peace of mind, but there was nothing here to comfort him. He picked up a stone and threw it into the next field. At the last minute he pulled back from kicking the tree, instead spinning round and lowering himself into a sitting position, his back against the tree trunk.

His mind dazzled him with pictures of Melody and himself, laughing, walking along together in wonderful countryside, peace and harmony between them. The image was so strong now he felt he could step into this place and disappear. This, he knew, was the edge of madness.

A small inner voice was also there, reminding him of another direction. It had no pictures to give, just a dark unknown, a horrific bike journey and an impossible task. There was no comfort in this direction, no green fields and sunny days to imagine. Just an odd sense, a seed of deep inner peace inside himself. He felt as though he had lived a thousand lives and only now was sure that such a deep feeling of peace was real and obtainable.

How could he leave everything? The school needed him. He was just ready to go into a wonderful relationship with Melody. This directionless journey was just stupid.

The thought of going on a long cycle ride left him feeling sick. He was afraid of very few things, but facing up to this particular part of his past was something he did not want to do. Conflicting emotions stormed through him. He knew one thing though - now was the time to decide. He also understood that no decision was also a decision.

He had a picture in his head of the many earth lives he had gone through. It was this idea that made the difference. He had always pursued the earthly pleasures and always had the same results. Time and time again he had taken the usual way, the path of life which seemed to fit best. He could not let go of this sense of inner peace, no matter where it took him. This was something deep inside of him, which he would lose unless he followed his intuition. He paused and looked back again. If he imagined all those people from all his past lives looking at him now, would they say, "Stay", or would they say, "Go"? There was really only one answer, the answer he did not like.

He thought it was funny. Wasn't that always the case with intuition? If you were going to do something anyway, then your intuition never put in an appearance. It only seemed to switch on to tell you to do something you did not want to do. He sighed, the way forward becoming clear.

He would pursue the adventure.

The emotions still raged through him but it was already different now. Having made his decision, his passions were not going to lead him astray. He could begin the process of calming himself now. Cameron shut his eyes and focused his attention on the space in the middle of his body where his heart was.

He sat very still, the profound shock to his mind resisting movement. He felt humbled. His inner conflict had gone, his dreams and wishes shattered. Cameron was left admiring the simple matters of life, the wonder of this beautiful world all around him. He was touched by something fundamental. Tears began to drop on his cheek as he acknowledged the silent wonder of creation and life. He was glad to be alive, even if he didn't know where life was taking him. But wasn't that always the case: no one ever knew which path of life on which they would travel. When this storm had moved on, the air would feel fresh and clear. In the same way, the storm in his mind and the junk in his head were also clearing. He began to stretch his body, one limb at a time before standing up. He looked back up at the storm, put the palms of his hands together in front of him and bowed down to the majesty of the tempest and the world around him.

Cameron turned round and began to walk back. He knew what to do, now.

14

Looking for the Heart of Paris

Cameron sat on a concrete block looking upriver. He had been to Paris several times before but never on his bicycle. His whole body ached, legs with hard muscles, arms sore, hands callused from grasping the handlebars all day long.

It had not been a long journey to get to the outskirts of Paris. He had spent four days traveling through England down to Dover in brilliant autumn sunshine, almost perfect weather for cycling. He loved the English countryside, the hedgerows, fields, grazing sheep and dotted trees spread throughout. The ferry from Dover to Calais was uneventful and even the security check in Calais went smoothly, the Police there being used to British cyclists.

Once he began moving south of Calais, the weather started changing. The sun disappeared behind a layer of dull grey cloud, which let loose occasional rain showers. Whereas in England it had been easy to find bed and breakfasts, in northern France the small hotels were not so accommodating to lone English riders and he had had more than one door closed in his face.

One episode in particular stuck in his mind. He was traveling on a busy road through the countryside when he observed three boys in the field next to the road setting up a sky-zapper machine, their bicycles dropped in the field around them. The zapper was about five meters in diameter, and it looked like a huge satellite dish, with a spherical bowl facing upwards and a long arm extending up its centre towards the sky.

He stopped for a while and watched them. He waved when they noticed him and they waved happily back. Sleepers seldom used sky-zappers and tended not to notice Heart People, so their waves were a mutual acknowledgement from the heart.

The boys had reached the point where the machine was fully unfolded and set up. They harnessed the rear wheel of one of their bicycles to a drive shaft, and started to pedal furiously to crank up the machine. The zapper started turning round on its axis. After a few minutes one of the boys flicked a switch and the dish started to sway from side to side, like a dynamo balancing on a string. They did not have to pedal so much now, just top it up now and again.

Cameron rested his bike at the side of the road and went across to speak to them. "Hello, ça va? How's it going?"

"Très bien Monsieur, it is bon, our machine, very good, n'est-ce pas?" The tallest of them came across and shook his hand, grinning from ear to ear, knowing his mixture of French and English would sound strange. "Mon ami, très vite, numéro cinq, all of France."

This was brilliant! Cameron remembered the background to the machines. A senior student from the Boston Heart Voyance School had seen the sky zappers being presented by its inventor at M.I.T. No one was taking up the zappers, despite their efficient simplicity. You pointed the machines up to the sky, got them running, and after an hour they had removed up to eighty percent of the air pollution for which they were designed. They were effective for up to a five kilometer radius.

The student took it on as a project and transformed their usage. He persuaded the inventor to build small, easy to transport zappers, such as the one the boys were using. Then, with a special site on the Net, each group could see what effect their efforts were having and where best to use them, using a pollution map. It did not take long before many youth groups took up the challenge and started using the machines, purchased by their local communities. For this group to reach the position of fifth best in France must have taken a lot of enthusiasm. And pedaling.

"Which gas are you working on?" asked Cameron.

"Gaz carbonique, how you say, carbon oxygen?"

"Carbon Dioxide? Number five in France? Wow, that is some achievement. Is it just the three of you?"

"Non, we are twelve, all from the same village."

"Have you got any more machines for other gases?"

"After we number three in France we get another machine. Then we get to the top five with that one too!" The other boys were calling him over now, so he turned round and ran to the bike. It was his turn to pedal.

"That's really great, très bien, mes amis!" said Cameron, reaching the limits of his French. He took his leave from them and with a last wave, he hopped back on his bike and continued his journey.

At first he was given a real boost by seeing the zapper in action. He felt a moment's contentment in being part of an international community whose very purpose was to put such projects into the world. But then he became dismayed - what was he thinking of, doing this bicycle journey, leaving all that behind?

Getting into Paris had been a chore. There were several police checkpoints. Getting his passport out and having his rucksack checked was not the problem. Trying to convince the Police why he was traveling on his own through France when, "everyone knew how dangerous the open roads were nowadays," that was the difficulty. His biggest problem was that he was a bad liar and yet he could not possibly tell the truth. Oh yes officer, I am cycling through your country as I have this odd idea that somewhere or other I am going to find a skull made out of quartz, perhaps just lying on the ground like lost treasure in a story long ago, and that I am going to pick it up and, well, very sorry, I don't have a clue what to do with it once I have found it, officer, but I will think of something once I get to that point.

Four security checks meant that he had taken a whole day to get from the outskirts of the city into the centre. The first police road block was two meters inside the Dome. It looked like a random position but it was put where the city police felt comfortable, and that was just inside the Dome.

He was exhausted. Physically, getting used to cycling again had been strenuous. Every night he seemed to ache in different parts of his body, and he had difficulty walking after spending a full day in the saddle. He tried to see the funny side of this and he had several jokes going through his mind at night when reviewing how sore his bottom was.

His main problem, though, was mental exhaustion. In the first few days of the journey, every time a lorry passed him just a little too close, he would feel a panic. Once, when cycling along an isolated French country road, a lorry overtook so close he felt he had to move to the side of the road to stop the rear of the vehicle clipping him. Cameron fell off his bike onto a grass verge and screamed. Raw fear swelled up inside him. He sat up, panting, head down. He had a slight graze on his arm but was otherwise physically unharmed, only shaken up. It seemed that every time a large vehicle went past Cameron heard the screams of his wife as she went under the wheels to her death. The fear was perhaps irrational. But that did not stop the screaming in his head. It continued for a long time.

Now he needed a place to rejuvenate. The Dome made his fears harder to deal with. He had become very aware of the Domes. He cycled through the country, then hit a Dome, country, Dome, country, then Dome. This experience highlighted the effects of the Domes and the artificial Dome/country, black/white construction. He had more sympathy for the Sleepers now. Was this what they had to go through every day of their lives? At least he knew how to recover his equilibrium.

Cameron cycled straight to the centre of the city. He found a small hotel in a side street and left his bike and belongings there. Going straight back out he headed down to the banks of the River Seine. There he sat for a while, before getting up and walking across to a small bronze plate against the side of a concrete wall. The plate commemorated the spot where Jacques de Molay had been burnt at the stake in 1314. Leader of the Knights Templar, he had fallen foul of the King and the Pope, who both attacked the Knights at the same time. There were so many secrets rumored to have been kept by that Order, yet all their mysteries went to the grave with the Knights or were lost to fables. Those that confessed under torture were later on found to have lied or imagined their confessions freely. He wondered what it would have been like to have lived at that time and to have led the order. What produced such dedication amongst all the Knights? Were they so devoted to God that they were willing to undergo torture and death so as not to break their vows?

Jacques de Molay had confessed under torture, a confession he later withdrew, a decision that cost him his life. Legend had it that he asked to die turned towards the cathedral of Notre Dame, being tied to the stake in such a way that he could hold his hands together in prayer.

He showed such utter devotion to his beliefs right up to the end of his life. There seemed to be so much belief in previous times. The great movers and shakers seemed always to belong to another golden age when it was so clear what was right and what was wrong. The fight for good was so much easier then, it was obvious what you were fighting for and what you were fighting against.

Cameron wondered what Jacques de Molay would have thought of his own quest. Riding on a bicycle through France without a clue as to where he was going, only that he was after a crystal skull. It must look easier when you are up there in the Heavens and can see the whole picture. Perhaps Jacques was smiling down on him, amused at the strange acts of incarnate human beings. Did de Molay have a good sense of humor? You never learnt that sort of thing from history books.

Cameron could not see the whole picture. He could not even see the day ahead. He was on this journey to the unknown on a used bicycle with only a backpack and panniers for company. He could only move further south, following a picture of a crystal skull that seemed to exist only in his mind. He had occasional images of a typical French château, so at least he knew he did not have to go to the ends of the Earth. His final destination was in this country. Somewhere within France he would find a château with a crystal skull in it. But what would he do when he got there? The place would be guarded. If a crystal skull was so important, it was hardly going to be left in the rubbish or accidentally forgotten at the roadside. How would he retrieve it? What would he do with the thing even if he got hold of it? Who should have the right to look after such an object?

These things kept on going round and round in his mind.

Did Jacques de Molay have such doubts? He still managed his affairs so that the Templar secrets remained undiscovered and provided future generations with a great wealth of intrigue and half-truths on which to speculate almost endlessly.

Here at the side of the river, Jacques was forgotten. This place had no memory of Jacques de Molay, at least none that he could find. The horrors of the deeds done here had been washed clean away by the river.

Cameron moved on to the cathedral. He joined a queue of tourists, paying his entrance fee and going into the building through the security scanner. Notre Dame no longer contained any special atmosphere either, just like at the riverside. The essential quality of the church built up by years of sincere worship had all been destroyed long ago by the flood of tourists lining up the aisles to gaze at the few strange believers left trying to pray to God. There was nothing left of the wealth of centuries of heartfelt prayer, the high atmosphere created by the devotion. Just the empty sound of the electronic turnstiles, the Church's coffers being filled by those lining up at the entrance.

He went outside and drifted around, looking for the heart of the city, heading almost inevitably for Montmartre. There in the Sacré-Coeur Basilica, he finally found the sustenance he was seeking.

The great church still had a holy atmosphere. There were notices at the main entrance asking people to be quiet for the sake of those who wished to pray, and the majority of visitors were conducting themselves accordingly. He sat down on one of the chairs but it did not feel right. He got up and explored further. He went down the stairs into the crypt. There, beneath the high altar was another altar, with a small cross, accompanied by two burning candles, and about twenty chairs in rows in front of it. There he found his place to pray.

Cameron sat down and made himself comfortable. He started repeating the Lord's Prayer over and over again in his mind. He used the shortened version of the prayer that was to be found in the original bibles, not the longer version more commonly spoken. Using this version in its Heart-Thinking form helped to strengthen its effect. Gradually he felt a calmness descend on him. He relaxed and opened himself up to take in the nature of the place.

There was a peaceful and relaxing quality here which seemed to fill his heart. He bathed himself in it, letting it flow through him, so no part of him, body, mind or spirit, remained untouched. He lost himself to it, almost falling asleep in the process. He kept his eyes wide open though, staring at one of the candle flames.

Once again he prayed hard, asking for strength and guidance. He felt a shiver go down his spine. This was his answer.

Cameron felt his strength returning. He rose and walked out, ready to start the next phase of his journey.

15

Leaving

Elaine thought that the only thing worse than standing watching the rain was standing watching the rain while waiting for a bus that was late, especially when you were running away. She wondered how long it would take them to discover she had gone. Would their special abilities enable them to notice she had left even before she had got out of town?

Cameron's leaving had really disturbed her. He was her main connection to the school, the main reason for coming here in the first place. She had not had much chance to see him at first but that did not lessen the bond she felt she had with him. With Cameron suddenly disappearing, her normal teenager hormones left her feeling homeless and she knew she had to get away.

She knew where she wanted to go. All she had to do was get on this bus without being seen.

A figure came around the corner of the street to her left, walking down the road through the rain in a black full-length cape, a small rucksack over one shoulder, heavy black eye-makeup peaking through stringy wet hair. She had not seen any Goths since arriving in Castleton and was a bit surprised to see one now. As Elaine continued to stare, she had the feeling she knew who it was. Could this be Malika? If it was Malika, why had she turned from a swan into a dreary Goth?

When Elaine was sure it was her, she turned round to walk off in the other direction. As soon as she faced up the road she saw Plume walking towards her, grinning. Looking across the road, there was Jason, also grinning. She was trapped. She turned and scanned Malika up and down.

"Is it going to take three of you to drag me back to school?"

The three of them moved together, each about one meter from the other. All three of them were facing into the centre, standing just to one side of Elaine. They stood there for about five seconds. Elaine thought something had passed between them, as if they had had a conversation at the speed of light. Clearly, as they moved out of the formation, there was a look of understanding between them. Had she imagined it? She put the thought aside as Malika turned to face her.

"Dear heart, did you seriously think you could get out of this place without half the town having at least some sort of inkling of what is happening to you? We are a heart-community, and when one heart is beating out of tune we all feel it. Cameron's departure was difficult for all of us but in the class we noticed your crisis too. So here we are."

"You are going to have to tie me up and drag me back."

"Listen pal, we might not look like knights in shiny amour, but that's what we are," replied Jason, a happy grin decorating his face. "One to the right, one to the left, Malika's ugly face to take the lead and scare any wrongdoers away. We're not here to take you back. We're going with you."

"Is there none better than I who knows how to take flight?" said Plume. "You might be ready to fly up and down like an albatross but with two hawks and a swan around you'll be aloft in mighty good company. And this flight will be a good jolly."

"Won't the school go bonkers when four pupils going missing?" asked Elaine.

"Dear Heart," said Malika. "When we saw what was up with you, Ginny and I sat down and thought about what to do. It's dangerous for you to go back into a Dome at the minute, you have changed a great deal since you used to live in London. You have opened yourself up and you could easily lose yourself in there. On the other hand, it's obvious your inner compulsion to go was something stronger than a desire to flee. You have some sort of a deed to fulfill, that's clear. So the only question was, how to help?

"So Ginny and I soon worked out that I would go as your guide. But I would not go alone. Plume and Jason might appear to be mentally challenged but their combined abilities will protect you through the cities. They will bubble-up. That is, they will form a protective bubble of energy around you in the Domes. Having two of them means they can keep topping you up, making sure the bubble never weakens. And, they are rather good at it. Without the bubble, you will find your passage through the Dome like walking through a full autumn storm. Except instead of wind, rain and wet leaves, you will be buffeted by emotions and fear.

"Once it was worked out what to do, Ginny and I went and told the teachers what was up. They listened to the plan, and with some minor modifications, agreed. We went and persuaded Plume and Jason and here we are."

"Talks good, don't she?" said Jason. "Note, she didn't even talk to us about going on a trip before she got the blessings from the teachers. We're just dragged from a class with so much as a, "D'ya fancy a quick jolly to Oxfordshire", just out yer pop, be on your way."

The small, twenty-seater bus appeared round the corner and after Malika put out her arm to signal, slowed down at the stop to pick them up. Elaine was lost, totally confused and had to be almost shoved on to the bus by Malika, now firmly in charge. They took their seats, Malika and Elaine side by side, Plume and Jason right behind them.

"But, I mean, Oxfordshire, I mean, how did you …' said Elaine, almost stuttering her words out.

"You were broadcasting your plans like a lighthouse in a winter's night, it was easy to pick out. Both Ginny and I are good at reading thoughts. When you first arrived, it made everyone feel better to know a new person would be living with Ginny. She could read you well. The only thing that confused us was your thoughts about Mole and your grandfather. We thought they were two different people and these two were so intermingled in your thoughts, we didn't understand. It was Melody who suggested checking whether they were one and the same person."

"But what were you doing, the three of you as you first stood at the bus stop? It was like you were talking but not talking. Was that telepathy or what?" asked Elaine.

Malika took in the change of subject with only a moment's pause. "It is a special technique. We thought together, with our hearts. The thought is one, though all three of us contribute to it. The thought was about our journey and how we would be doing it, who would be playing what roles, what the different options and decisions are. The thought built up instantly between us. It's alive, we can tap into it later if we need more help. It's a different way of thinking than what you are used to with your head."

"Isn't that what the teachers do? This Heart-Thinking?" asked Elaine.

"Yes, but we can do it really quickly. When we are older we'll be experts in a way the teachers cannot even conceive. They're getting quite good at finding ways of using it. For example, if they want to get together quickly, they will use Heart-Thinking to broadcast a request to those who are interested. Then they all appear. Much better than using technology. But the teachers are hampered by the overall backwardness of the consciousness in this country. That will have to change of course."

"How will that change?" asked Elaine again.

Malika's forehead creased as she looked back at Elaine. "Well dear heart, something tells me our current journey is going to make a great deal of difference, but I have no idea why. Now relax, we have a long but safe journey ahead of us."

*

Mole was rather surprised to open the solid oak door of his remote house to a rather sodden looking set of pupils. He didn't hesitate, dragging Elaine and the others indoors and kicking them upstairs for a shower and a change of clothing before they all sat down on the sofa in front of the fire. Elaine's favorite toast with sour cherry jam appeared as if by magic. He asked them all sorts of questions about the school and the journey, which they all did their best to answer without spitting bits of toast back at him. The questions about Cameron were frequent. Mole was not bothering to hide the fact that he was very interested in him.

They could stay for a few days, that much was clear to everyone. The house was a sizeable mansion and there was room enough for everyone. Mole insisted a message be sent to the school, informing them that the four pupils were fine and in safe hands.

Tired, Elaine settled into her usual bed that night, quite content. She had new friends who had accompanied her all this way. How could Malika read her so easily? In the same way she knew exactly what to do with computers, without a doubt. Jason and Plume kept themselves to themselves, but they were quite aware of her the whole journey. They had already made plans for the next day. Jason would examine the energy structures of the land around the house and Plume would check out the bird life. The two of them would then get together and explore the connections between the two. If they found any interesting facts, for example, the type of land energy to be found where particular birds liked to nest, then they wanted to present it back at school. In fact, they were so confident of success, they were already planning the presentation.

That was something else Elaine noticed about her fellow pupils. They were very self-confident. It was not just a front, they really were self-assured.

This was a strange new world in which she found herself. She had wanted to run away but the school had come along with her in the form of her eccentric companions. She felt safe and yet did not know what would happen next, which was awesome. Happy to have made it this far, she settled down to a contented sleep

16

A Night Out

Cameron pulled to the side of the road and got off his bike. The steep hill was too much for him on his fully loaded bike. He paused and looked around him. On both sides of the road lay rolling hills with the white tips of the Alps just visible above the skyline on the left. A long incline rose before him, going up forever. Both sides of the hill were covered in evergreen trees. In the fading light of the afternoon, the woods appeared dark and uninviting.

He had been thinking all day about how much money he had and came to the conclusion he would have enough for twelve more nights in a hotel. The problem was, he had no idea how long the journey would take to get to wherever he was going. Then he had the problem of cycling all the way back. He sat down for a rest and thought about his situation.

After leaving Paris he had traveled south for about twenty kilometers and then started heading on the road due east. He still had no idea where he was going and was rather surprised at the change of direction. He had arrived at a large junction just after leaving Paris and expected to just continue going south. However, when he left the junction by the southern exit, his heart started expanding and he saw pictures of himself cycling off left, in the easterly direction. He tried to continue cycling further south, but it was as if his heart was tugging him back up the road. It did not leave him in peace.

Turning the bike round, he cycled back up to the junction and turned onto the eastbound road. Only then did his heart return to its muted state.

Reflecting on this moment made him realize he was now totally committed to following his heart. He had no other way of judging what was the best direction to pursue. Although he had been using and refining his intuitive ability for years, he had always had the choice as to whether to heed it or not. Now, in this situation, he had committed himself to using his ability for the whole of the journey, without knowing what was to unfold. If he did not obey his heart he might as well just turn round and cycle home, greet his friends and pretend he had just been on an unexpected holiday.

Instead he had continued cycling for nine days through the rolling countryside before ending up in the Rhine valley. He rode through picturesque old wine villages dotted around the foothills of the Vosges mountain range. In the villages the farmers still setup roadside stalls where you could buy their produce and leave your payment in old fashioned coins in a little cash box. In this way he had munched his way through pounds of apples.

Continuing to follow his intuition, he cycled up a steep hill to Mount St. Odile. Here were the ruins of an abandoned abbey, now turned into a museum. He also found further spiritual sustenance at the hilltop, though not in the small church nor in the souvenir shop. Outside on the far side of the mountain, just at the edge of a cliff, he found three holes cut into the solid rock. The tourist information labelled them as graves, for they were as large as coffins and shaped in human form. He wondered about this. The mountain had a special atmosphere. It would be a typical place where, in the hidden centuries, the mystics would have settled and performed their rites. The graves looked like the place where initiates would be buried for three days. After the third day, the stone covering the hole containing the initiate would be rolled aside. If the initiate had survived, they would have sat up and seen the most gorgeous panorama of the whole of the Rhine valley spread out before them, visible from this open place on the hillside. After having lived in darkness for three days, such a sight must have filled them with awe of the wonders of the universe and the beauty of this planet.

This was another moment which kept him going. In some ways he wondered if he was progressing through a magical tour of the special mystical sites of France. Or was this just the spiritual sustenance he needed to keep going, to know that others had been through much worse trials than this?

Because he needed the sustenance. It was easy for those old initiates. They would have trained for years to face their challenge. When they stood in the trial alone, at least they knew that their friends and colleagues were nearby.

Cameron was so aware of being alone. He had had very few conversations throughout his journey, and most of those were superficial, just, "Hello, une baguette s'il vous plaît." His French was limited and although international English was heard in the towns, it was little used in most of the villages through which he traveled. This lack of personal contact with people affected him more than he expected. He realized just how much sustenance he received from those who knew and respected him.

Here, in the towns, people were unfriendly. It was noticeable that there were Domes around some very small places. Has the division in humanity become so exact that such a strict separation was necessary? How then were Heart People going to help Sleepers progress? This question went in deeper than Cameron realized.

After Mount St Odile, he followed the Rhine valley south, pausing at Colmar. Cameron had never been to this place before. He was enchanted. There was a modern centre serving the town and the surrounding countryside, and an old quarter filled with half-timbered houses, fully renovated, to the delight of the throngs of tourists. There, in this mix of waterside wildlife, tree, plants and old buildings steeped in history, he felt at home. He would have loved to have known the history of so many of these timber framed black and white houses; who built them, what ideas did they aspire to, what hopes did they have for their construction? Who lived in them through the hundreds of years since they were built? What lives passed within? These were things that he longed to be able to investigate.

He continued towards Basel and then south-west through France, going round the foothills of the Jura until he arrived at his current position, a few kilometers north of Geneva. The last part of the journey he had not enjoyed. Some people traveled a long way to come to this part of the world on holiday. Cameron found it oppressive though, and would have been quite happy never to see the place again.

It was at that point that he had his second accident. There was very little traffic on the back roads. A lorry overtook him along the narrow roads, forcing him to sway away from the road. The weight of the panniers pulled him off his balance and he fell onto the embankment at the side of the road. He lay there for a moment, just moving slightly to see if anything was damaged. This time only his pride was hurt. He laughed at the absurdity of the situation, lying on the grass at the side of the road looking up at the sky on a journey without destination.

The peace of nature was disturbed by the oncoming chug, chug, chug sound of an approaching tractor. It was traveling along a field track and arrived at the road only five meters from his restful entanglement.

The tractor was a simple, old-fashioned farm workhorse driven by a middle aged man in blue overalls. Sitting on a seat placed just above one of the large wheels, a young boy, about ten years old, was traveling with him.

The boy was dressed in a dark jacket and jeans, his pale face surrounded by wild corkscrew red hair. He started yammering at the driver and waving one hand in Cameron's direction. The driver stayed where he was but with a well-practiced leap, the boy jumped down and ran across to Cameron. The boy started talking in accented French as he bent down to help Cameron up. Cameron shook his head and said in English he didn't understand. The boy pointed to his left leg and patted the knee twice. Cameron understood he was to lift up this leg and as he did so, the boy, struggling with the weight, pulled the bike off him and stood it upright on its stand. Cameron was still struggling to his feet when the boy grasped his hand and pulled him up.

Cameron tried to speak his thanks again but the boy just continued his stream of French. Realizing that the man did not understand, the boy pointed animatedly at his mouth with one finger. From his pocket he pulled out a sandwich in a plastic wrapping and pushed it at Cameron.

Cameron was moved by the generosity. He looked across to the man on the tractor who gave a curt nod of approval. Cameron took the offered food. The boy grinned, ran back to the tractor and with a quick climb back onto his seat, was away with a wave. Cameron looked at the sandwich and smelt it. Salad with Alsatian Munster cheese, not his favorite, too smelly for his taste. He stuck the sandwich in a back pocket, climbed back on his bike and continued his journey.

The sun passed behind the hill. After a few more hours he realized the sun had set, the color fanfare obscured behind light grey cloud. In the fading light he found a small copse of trees. He placed his bike against a tree, on the inside of the little wood, where it could not be seen from the road. He used his rucksack as a pillow, leaving the panniers on the bike. He took out a light sleeping bag and an inflatable ground sheet. He got into the sleeping bag fully clothed to keep warm and lay down.

It was not quite dark but he wanted to get an early start the next day, so he was happy to go to sleep now. It was a shame the stars were not shining, but at least the clouds did not look dangerous. He did not want to wake up feeling like a soggy sandwich in the morning. He closed his eyes and dozed off.

The sound of whispering voices woke him up. Cameron shook his head and tried to sit up, disorientated in the dark, not knowing where he was. A torch-light came on a few meters away. He shouted in response to the light hitting his face and blinding him. There was a metallic noise recognizable as belonging to a bike. He realized someone was trying to steal his bicycle, and stood up to try and stop them, shouting incoherently in English. The response was muffled laughter coming from young voices retreating towards the road, the light switched off, the clicking of the rear bike wheel indicating his property was departing with them. He was still in his sleeping bag and furiously tried to push it down over his legs before setting off in pursuit. He stepped forwards, not realizing that the sleeping bag was still wrapped around one foot. He lost his balance and fell over, his head hitting something hard.

When he came to consciousness again, the bleak light of early morning enabled him to look around. Underneath his head, like a rough pillow, was a half rotten log. His sleeping bag was still entangled around one leg, the other part of it trailed away through muddy grass.

His bike was gone, the panniers and contents with it. He only had his rucksack and the soggy clothes he stood up in. He patted his jacket pockets happy to feel his wallet with his documents inside. Well, at least his ID and cash cards were safe, so he could still travel.

If life was an ongoing rollercoaster of ups and downs, then Cameron was now at the bottom of a deep loop. His energy was gone, he had nothing left. With no motivation, there was just a yawning emptiness inside. He knew, the real power and inspiration for human deeds came from within. But here he had nothing more to give. As much as he did not want to go home a failure, he had no other choice. He was at the end.

He put his rucksack on his back, picked up his muddy sleeping bag and ground sheet and began the slow walk into the next town. The sleeping bag dragged carelessly on the ground and was deposited in the first garbage bin that he came across.

It took him half an hour to reach the town. It was a typical small border community. The real heart of such a place was in the city across the border, and an excess of time or spirit was not given to this local community. The houses were grey and non-descript, the place impossible to remember after having left it. He had been walking through the streets for ten minutes before he realized he had forgotten the town name.

It left his spirits sinking even lower. Even the idea of going home filled him with no desire or hope. It was not a goal; he just had no idea what else he should do.

He looked up, searching the surrounding hills for the beauty of Mother Nature to refresh him. This was when he spotted it.

The hills to the East rose well above a thousand meters and would soon be topped in snow. On the other side of the valley, half way up the slope of the nearest peak, was a small château, half-hidden by the surrounding wood. It had two small round turrets with pointed roofs, and tall surrounding walls made out of sandstone, rising out of the rock of the hillside. The impression it left on him was one of cold foreboding.

At the same moment as he saw the château, his heart area went clear.

Awareness came to him: this was his destination, the place he would find the crystal skull.

Cameron stood still looking at the château for a while before turning and going further into the town. He stopped at the next bakery and went in. As he bought a baguette he tried asking the shop assistants about the château. They were reluctant to answer and he learnt nothing but how unpleasant unsmiling faces are. His next attempt at conversation at the counter of the local supermarket brought more success in the form of a talkative young woman. With persistence he found out that the château belonged to a banker who worked just across the border in Geneva. The banker kept a low profile and the locals had little to do with the château. There was one odd fact; the château was new, less than twenty years old! It had been built on the rock outcrop and designed to look four hundred years old. Was this a modern day folly, built on the whim of the vain rich?

Cameron took his bread and ate his improvised breakfast while sitting on a bench in a small park. He thought over what to do. He could hardly just walk up to the front door in daylight and ask for the crystal skull back. The only alternative that came to mind was to sneak up at night. They must have the latest infrared security, and the chances of a mouse entering the château without them knowing must be small. Armed security personnel, trained guard dogs were the least to expect. Well, walking straight up to the château at night was what he had in store and once there he would find out what would happen. After all, they could not do more than turn him away. Could they?

The whole idea filled him with cold stillness, like a winter fog. He did not want to disappear here in this far-flung place without anyone familiar knowing where he was and what he was going to do.

He walked into a small café and in stuttering English and French got them to understand that he wanted to use a standard Net portal. This was a very strange thing to do, he realized, but something told him not to use his own. Instead of vocalizing his message he sat down and typed it in. This did not bring any reaction from the waiter so he guessed that they were used to people keeping their messages private. The message was to Melody. He told her which town he was in, checking the name on top of the Com. In a few short sentences he told her he was going to go to the château on the hill that evening and he was not sure what would happen. At the last minute, just before he sent it, at a whim he copied Elaine in on the message as well.

That was it. All he had to do now was sit around waiting for nightfall. Perhaps then he would simply walk up the hill and be stopped by a security guard. Perhaps not. His stomach muscles were knotted with the tension and he felt sick.

Cameron bought more water and sandwiches to keep him going for the next twenty-four hours. He walked back out of town to the copse of trees where he had slept the night before. After he set his alarm clock for 11:00pm, he lay down with his head nestling in the roots of an old oak tree. Cameron shut his eyes and prayed, with all his might, for courage. With a mixture of relief and mercy, he fell into a dream.

17

Elaine Attacks

Malika opened the door, striding in as if she was the Lady of the House.

"Ever practiced knocking?" said Elaine,

"You are right, dear heart, I have to practice my entrances. Something less dramatic would be more appropriate. I do like the theatrical in every day life, though it makes it all so much more fun!

"Now is your time. You have to go. Now!"

"Malika, we have been here for two days and you have been quite happy to sit around and enjoy doing as little as possible. All of a sudden, you want to leave?"

"No, no, I don't want to go anywhere. It's time for you to go down to the machine room where Mole works and do your stuff there. I don't know what it is, but there is a task for you to do, something only you can do, and the time is now. I have an oppressive

170

feeling in my heart and this is not going to shift until you get down there and discover what you are here for."

Elaine looked at her sceptically. "Malika, Mole has some of the greatest Net experts in the country in and out of here on a constant basis. They reek of competence. There is no way I can be better than them at something."

"Well, there is something you can do better, that is the reason why you are here. And the only way to know is to go downstairs and find out. What d'you say?"

"If you're so clever why don't you go?"

"My skill is with people. Yours is with machines. Do you not understand? Only you can do this. Now will you please go?"

Elaine gave in, throwing a jumper over her shoulders. She made her way down to Camp X, as Mole called the machine room where he worked. She went and sat at a Com, gazing at the screen and occasionally looking over devotedly at Mole. She was happy to be in his company, feeling safe and excited at the same time. Things always happened when Mole was around.

She remembered a time when she was here before. Ivan was often here then, a tall, lanky figure who had his own desk at which he could stand up. He had dark straggly hair and an unkempt beard, which he twisted in his fingers when he was thinking. He was a specialist in Eastern European languages, and had been rooting through the Moldavian defense systems when he hit jackpot. He discovered the project plans for the military's build up of biological weapons. The team gathered round and read the translations before deciding together on appropriate action: they dropped them in the inbox of MI6 with a short note to say that they had put out an unstoppable post so that two weeks later it would span out to Net News. That got the spies into action.

It was fun here. She knew, though, that sooner or later Mole would get round to persuading her to go back home or to school and that she would not be able to say no. But for now she was in a peaceful oasis.

There were several others in the room with her. Snowy she also knew from previous visits. Mole was over in a corner speaking to a short rotund woman who went by the Net name of Skinny. Elaine was looking for things to do and went and checked her inbox. That was when she found the message from Cameron. She looked at it for a second and was just about to call Mole over when she re-read it. Mole had always taught her to check everything twice. Then she had to wait a few minutes before Mole freed himself from Skinny's attention and could come over and read the mail. Elaine repeated how Cameron left the Heart Voyance School under strange circumstances, which caused her instant flight.

"So Cameron went away on a journey on his bike," said Mole. "What was he trying to solve? What did he want to accomplish?"

She explained how the school could not operate under the new rules and faced closure. "There was also something else but I did not quite understand. The school had just installed a new energy motor. A V-Gen. I heard the teachers talking about it. They've got problems getting a patent and they wanted to do something through the schools in America, but I didn't understand what."

Mole looked at her the whole time, giving her his full concentration. Elaine looked back at him, waiting for him to respond. "That explains quite a bit," he said. "I wondered why the new government were trying to control the private schools. It didn't make sense. The people in those schools will create a fuss if you try and force them to do something they don't want to, so attempting to control them is like trying to move a beehive - if you don't have protective clothing or a very thick skin, you risk getting severely stung."

"But what's all that got to do with the U.S.?" asked Elaine.

"I would guess the V-Gen is an invention of the Heart Voyance School College," answered Mole. "They have three small colleges, one in the Yorkshire Dales, another in California and a third in New Zealand. They have a dual role of training new teachers and doing their own research, sort of like a small university. In each country, the colleges are connected to the schools in a loose administrative framework. So if they are having patent difficulties here, they can easily ask the schools in the U.S. to put a patent through. Even easier for them would be to do it in New Zealand.

"You see, energy is the most sensitive issue we have at this time. As soon as they apply for a patent then they are announcing to the world that they are active in this area. The thinking in the Anglo-Saxon world is still very confused on this issue and it would be easy to upset some powerful people. These people would do everything they could to stop such a machine ever being put into production. It would ruin their monopoly on energy resources and in one stroke remove their power base. They could not allow that. It might be easier to put the patent through in the U.S. where the government is more open than ours, even if the country is just as chaotic. Better would be New Zealand where they are desperate to have any gain in energy efficiency.

"But getting back to Cameron, let's see what we can find out about this château he is going to break into, shall we?" Mole set to work on the terminal, setting forth a variety of verbal commands. Elaine recognized some of them as common search routines but others she had no idea what they were doing. Mole was keeping six different windows going, quickly typing commands into each window, saving his voice for Elaine, giving her a running commentary of what he was doing.

"First we have to trace the email back to the terminal it was sent from. That's not so difficult, the email itself contains the numbers of all the computers it traveled through. We get the ID number of the ending computer and then find out where that number is located. Here it is, Champfromier, in France. Let's look a bit closer at this town. Google shows us lots of pictures of the village but none of a château. That's odd, you would have thought that the château would be one of the more prominent features of the village. Let's have a look at some of the other image engines. Nothing. Now that's very odd.

Hey, Snowy, ever traced through Google whether any photos have been forcibly removed? I am looking at the town of Champfromier in France, about sixty kilometers from Geneva. We're wondering why we can't see any pictures of its château."

Snowy looked across, a puzzled expression creasing his face up. "That name sounds familiar, let's take a look," he said, walking across to Elaine and Mole. "I know that place, I'll just check." Snowy went back to his own computer and started typing. After a very short time he stopped, looked across at them and made his announcement. "You have found a Golden Coffin. It's no wonder you don't have any pictures of the château. It is owned by one Marcus de Brey. Like all those involved with the Golden Coffins, it is extremely difficult to find out any details about them. Even the tax office has little to say about them. What do you want with that château?"

Mole quickly explained the situation with Cameron. "If we can break into their house Com, maybe we can tweak the security systems in Cameron's favor," said Mole.

"Hmm, we can break into almost any system in the world but their security we have never got through," said Snowy. "Remember, we traced the single landline into their building and have snooped the IO, but have never been able to crack their security."

"Any ideas what sort of system it could be?" asked Mole.

"Either it is something so high tech we have never heard of it or it is something so primitive we cannot see it. It seems to be time based. All the handshake signatures alter every time we look at it."

"We know every security system ever made, including a few put together in this building. I find it strange to think we can't crack this one. Are these guys so sophisticated that they know something we don't? What's your opinion, Snowy?"

"There is something so incredibly odd about having just one landline in and no wireless. My guess is this is something really old fashioned. I can't figure it out."

"But I can," jumped in Elaine. Her whole face was lit up and she could hardly sit still. Snowy and Mole looked at her silently. She noticed their calmness, took a deep breath and continued slowly. "I know exactly how to break into this system. Bring up the trace on the IO to the landline and I will show you."

Mole and Snowy looked at Elaine but did not respond.

"I can do this," said Elaine. "You'll see. Let me try."

Mole looked at Snowy. "Let's see what she can do," he said.

18

Mole's Revenge

At first, nothing Elaine did seemed to work. She sat at the terminal and tried various different inputs. She spoke the codes and Mole typed them in and sent them to the Coffin. Nothing happened. It was only when Malika prompted them that they became successful. "You are losing too much in translation," she said. "Elaine is spouting out a whole range of ones and zeros but not all of them are going onto the computer correctly. You have to find a different way, something not so open to error."

"Use hexadecimal," said Snowy.

Elaine was directly alert, "What's hexadecimal?"

"Our normal number system works with numbers between zero and nine," said Snowy. "We count upwards and once we reach ten we add a one, getting one and zero to represent ten. Hexadecimal is a larger numbering system, counting numbers between zero and fifteen. To represent ten, eleven etc, we use the first letters of the alphabet, A, B, C and so on. Once we get to sixteen, we represent it with a one and zero. So one and zero in hexadecimal represents sixteen and in normal numbers represents ten. On computers you can quickly transfer between hexadecimal and binary. The hexadecimal is much easier to work with than binary too."

"Do you think you can you work with that?" asked Mole.

"Just a minute." Elaine closed her eyes tight shut for a minute. Then she quickly started spitting out a series of numbers and characters. "A. 4. 5. 0. E. 2. 4. C."

Mole typed it in and constructed his package to send to the Com and away it went. The response was immediate. "We're in. By God we've done it. We're in a Coffin.

"Snowy, I'm sending out on channel two. Can you split the signal and join in?" Snowy busied himself at his terminal.

"Got it. I'm in as well. Let's see what sort of a setup they have, how many walls we have to tunnel through."

Snowy and Mole worked intensively at the terminals for the next few minutes. A few words flew back and forth between them, nothing that Elaine or Malika could follow.

"Through," said Snowy.

"How many nodes?"

"Five, all parallel. Let's go for the key disk."

"That will be locked tighter than the Tower."

The short silence was disturbed by the sound of keyboards being hammered at. Snowy spoke first. "Christ, it's free! The idiots have nothing in place, it's wide open!"

"Sister nets? Can you jump to the other Coffins?"

"Wait!' shouted Elaine. Mole and Snowy looked up. "We didn't get in to fulfill your hacking dreams, we have to help Cameron."

"She's right," said Snowy.

"Can you find their security systems?" prompted Malika. Snowy looked across at her, as she continued. "What is your intuition telling you, where is the root of the security system?"

"Node four is where we would expect to find it," said Mole, interrupting the exchange.

"It's node two, it's a really old setup. These might be the Kings of the earth but they have a configuration that died off with Kernighan and Ritchie! It's no wonder we could never hack it, who could have guessed they were using such dinosaurs! This is freaky, it's giving me the collywobbles."

"Node two it is. Full old-fashioned menu system, no restrictions. I'll follow up with this. Snowy, let's get a full systems print here then you go marching to the sister nodes. Take the toolkit in with you, see what other physical access we can locate. If they only have one land line they might spot us."

"OK chucklebutty, let's map it out."

"Once you get that far then call out the rest of the troops. Better still, call them out now. Tell them what channel you are on and they can follow you in. Start with Wendy and Grey Wolf. Abdabs, Ivan and Farmer Giles to follow."

Mole worked furiously at the terminal for a few minutes before turning to Elaine. "Snowy will make a map of their systems. With that we can see exactly what they can do. I now have access to their building security system. It looks like they had an outer defense, which kept us at a distance but once through, all their systems are open to anyone. No further I.D. checks necessary. Stupid. Within the next thirty minutes Snowy will have complete control over their systems, assuming they don't spot us, which is unlikely.

"Now what do you think this Cameron will be doing?"

Malika answered the question instead. "He cannot just walk up to the door and hope to steal something. On the other hand, he has no idea about security and controls. I suspect he will do something daft like jump over the garden wall and under cover of darkness try to sneak in."

Mole looked at Elaine. She nodded, "Malika is a good judge of character and has known Cameron much longer than I have. That sounds pretty spot on to me."

"OK, that makes it easy. Snowy, how's the toolkit coming on?"

"Ninety percent loaded on node four. Port harnesses all ready there, if that's what yer after."

"Thanks." Mole continued talking as he typed away at his terminal. He soon had four windows open and was flicking between them, keeping a series of commands running on the distant machine. "So Elaine, we will take charge of the input feeds from their security cameras. As soon as it gets dark we will be able to feed them old pictures of nothing at all, that's what the port harnesses that Snowy is loading will do.

"Malika, would you be so kind and find out when dusk falls down in Geneva? We can then see how much time we've got left to set things up.

"Elaine, I'll look around and see if I can find the security schedules of the guards, see what time they patrol the premises. What I need you to do is look after the guard dogs. Once we have those under control we can pretty much guarantee Cameron access to the building. After that he is on his own.

"Hey Snowy, they have full infra red simulation here, have you still got that fox intruder simulation in the toolkit?"

"Yep, you going to cover his tracks?"

Mole looked back at Malika and Elaine grinning from ear to ear. "Snowy once wrote a simulation program that takes the video feed of a human shape and makes it appear like a fox. Before Cameron arrives we will have it installed on their infrared systems so that they never notice that a human being was there, just a marauding fox. If we get it right, there will be no electronic record of Cameron being in the building."

Snowy turned around and said, "Hey, Wendy and Peter Pan are on their way here. They want to be in on the cracking. They want to know who else they can call out and whether you have contacted the Green Knights?"

"Tell them they can contact any one of the Cleaners. I will contact the Knights as soon as we have access to the other coffins."

"I'm already there. Wendy hooked in as well. She's running from a portable now in a 'copter. I think she has others lined up behind her, I can't believe how quick she's progressing."

After that things started moving faster than Elaine and Malika could follow. Various faces and voices appeared across the terminals, the occasional laughter easing the tension in the room. One by one people trickled in. An older Indian couple came into the room. The woman had a vertical red mark in the middle of her forehead. Snowy grinned at her, "Watcha Wendy!" Elaine was surprised when Mole went up and gave a small bow of greeting to her. "Elaine, I would like you to meet my mentor, Wendy, one of the greatest hackers of the century." After short introductions they all resumed their places in front of the screens.

Soon there were over fifteen people in the room. Mole organized them into their groups. Amongst all these computer experts, Malika began to feel as if she had a non-speaking part in a radio play and slid out of the room. Mole relinquished control of the château's security to others, but not before Elaine had sorted out what to do with the guard dogs. That caused much merriment.

"Look there," exclaimed Snowy. "There's something happening on the south-west wall." Sure enough they could see a tree branch lying on top of the wall, moving from side to side. Snowy spliced in a video recording from twenty minutes previously showing the wall free from any foliage. Elaine was shocked at how quickly they had taken control of the château's systems. It was only now that she realized that Mole's circle of friends were some of the brightest hackers in the world.

"He's not going to get very far like that," said Mole. "Can we let him in any other way?"

"There is a small door just five meters to his right. We can unlock it from here. There's no way to tell him it is open."

"He will just have to find out for himself," said Mole.

"The château has another defense layer. Three meters inside the wall there's a ring of motion detectors that fire tranquilizing darts at anything that it detects. It's fully automated, has secondary battery power supply – it'll take a while to find out how to switch it off," said Wendy.

"How long have we got?" asked Elaine.

"Look," replied Snowy. "He has just found the door. Looks like we have run out of time. How deadly are those darts?"

"I wish I knew," replied Wendy.

19

The Untouchable

Melody was looking at the mail from Cameron. It was the first time she had heard from him in weeks and she was concerned. Something was wrong but she could not define it, and this irritated her. What was this situation he had got himself into? Why would going into a château generate such unease? Surely the worst that could happen was that he would be arrested for trespassing? There was a sense that she had to do something now, but what?

Restless, she went downstairs and wandered around the house. She found her husband lying on the sofa, snoring, a half-empty bottle of vodka standing on the floor, not far from his head. She picked up the bottle and carried it into the kitchen, emptying the contents into the sink. She returned to the lounge and looked at the unconscious figure draped across the sofa. A feeling of deep sadness engulfed her. It was part of their agreement that he would not drink at all, the alcohol increasing the potential for another violent outburst. She had made it very clear that with even one drink she would leave. Just to be sure, they had drawn up a written statement which they both had signed, with examples of what behavior they would not tolerate. Well, now he had made his choice and forced her hand. She could not help him anymore and was no longer going to try.

She went back upstairs and sat on the edge of the bed, the tears beginning to flow, the sobs following on quickly. There was nothing more she could do and this was the hardest thing for her to accept. It was her destiny to help others and this point blank refusal of help from someone she had loved was paralyzing. She started feeling a surge of emotions, brooding resentment, sudden thunders of anger, the muddy depths of hatred stirring up ...

She stopped. She was being swamped and she knew it. Melody was quite aware of the dangers of being with a Sleeper, getting lost in their turbulent, relentless emotions. Strange that now, just at the end, was when she was in most danger of losing herself. Had she lost her protection?

She turned her attention to herself, observed her breathing, in-breath, out-breath, the sound of her heart adding an extra rhythm. This calmed her down enough to detect a nagging memory. She had not done anything about Cameron's mail.

Focusing back on Cameron, the same feeling of urgency and danger persisted. Not knowing what to do left a clear idea of a way forward. She had to call a Gathering. She looked at her watch. It was 7:00 pm. A strange time to be drunk? She cast the thought aside and prepared to send out a message, calling for a Gathering at 8:00 pm. She concentrated on her heart and sent out the energy calling for help for Cameron, feeling herself open up as she did so. It became clear to her just how much her heart energy had wilted, being tied to a Sleeper. Renewed, she pushed out the energy further, awed at her own capability and power.

She put on her jacket and shoes, and closed the front door behind her as she made her way over to the school. She let herself into the small conference room, lit a candle, placed it at the window and waited.

It did not take long until someone appeared. Daniel was first, his tall thin frame filling in the door. He did not say a word, not even hello, but his warm smile was relaxing. He settled into a chair and they sat in comfortable silence. Jack and Lia arrived next, together with three other teachers. Then came the surprise.

In walked Centus and two other young men from the upper school. They confidently took their place at the table. Jack started to object but at that minute a voice spoke from the doorway, "Leave them be," said Cathy. "I think we are going to need all the help we can get and the young ones have already developed themselves well beyond our expectations." She looked across at Centus and the others. "Welcome."

Melody explained the situation to the Gathering. Cathy took charge and started organizing. While she was talking, Melody got up and slipped out. No one made any comment on her disappearance.

Cathy asked, "Lia, would you be so kind and go to the office and bring back a photo of Cameron, it will help us to concentrate."

When Lia came back she continued. "There are two things we can do for Cameron. The first is to bubble-up, good and proper, as if he was a Knight of old and we are putting him in amour. He must be energetically invincible. Centus, this is where the concentration ability of you and your friends can really help us.

"The other is to provide Cameron with as much ability as possible, everything he needs. This is not a clearly defined task. We need to use our Intuition to sense what he requires, and then provide him with as much as we can. That is for the rest of us to do."

They discussed this for a while and then divided into two groups. One would focus on Cameron's head, the other on his heart.

They were just about settled when Melody came back through the door, followed by Joel. There were some surprised faces amongst the teaching staff. Centus stood up and went to Joel, shook his hand, placing his other hand on his upper arm as he was doing so. "I am glad you are here, we need you."

Melody and Joel took their places at the table and were quickly brought up to date with the plans. A further set of explanations went backwards and forwards before Cathy spoke up, "O.K., I think it's time we got started."

They all went into silence. There was a small rustling of clothes as various people shuffled about until they found a position in which they could relax and concentrate their minds on Cameron.

The room became still. An atmosphere of intense concentration developed, as they all focused their minds on Cameron. For the pupils, this was an easy undertaking. They were familiar with the task and knew exactly what to do. At the same time the tension started building up amongst the teachers. Something was not happening correctly. It was as if something or someone knew what they were trying to do and was blocking them off, stopping anything getting through. The room started to feel hot and the air thick, as if a thousand candles were in the room using up the oxygen and replacing it with smoke. This scenario continued. The teachers were very proficient at concentrating; they could hold a thought for a long time. This feeling of not being able to get through, of being held back caused them to work harder. They were all focused, their minds fully engaged. It became clearer that they were hitting what felt like a smooth black wall, which seemed impenetrable. What could it be? They tried harder and harder but no one was left with the feeling that they were getting anywhere.

Suddenly Joel stood up. His movements were quick, and his chair fell back behind him. With his hands placed firmly on the table he leaned forward and with full force screamed, "Jump!", not stopping until his lungs were empty.

Chaos erupted around the table. They had their minds in full concentration on Cameron and the scream was an explosive attack. Most groaned, holding their heads in pain. It was an abrupt ending to the Gathering, being ripped out of their inner focus with such a violent noise. One of the friends of Centus went over to a waste paper bin and began quietly retching.

"I am sorry, it was a growing impulse, it had to be said. I tried to resist, I knew what damage it would do. The words had to come out and they had to be screamed. I don't know why but it had to be just so," said Joel.

Centus had his arm over his friend who was trying to regain his composure with deep breaths. "We understand. The question is, will it work?"

"For that, we will have to wait and see," replied Cathy

The Untouchable

20

The Château

Cameron looked up to the top of the hill. He thought it was after twelve o'clock but he was not certain. The château seemed impossibly far away. It had a large garden area surrounded by a simple looking stone wall about two meters high. The tall thin towers of the château could be seen outlined against the darker night sky, and lights were shining out of some of the thin upper windows. Here he was, on foot, in the middle of the night, aware that the darkness would provide no security against the surveillance equipment that would detect him.

One thing he knew though, he was not about to turn back. He remembered as a young boy reading a book about Richard the Lionheart. One scene in the book always remained with him. It was a picture of when King Richard, surrounded by the army, weary of the political infighting of the nobles, decided to abandon the Crusade and return home. Little did he know he was only a few miles away from the worn and broken army of Saladin, and that if he had moved forward just a short distance he would have won a decisive victory against the Muslim leader. Cameron was not sure how correct the book was, nor if it would have been a good idea if King Richard had continued, but it did not matter. The picture it left him was how by just going that one step further, not giving up no matter how impossible things might seem, the whole world can suddenly change. Just as would have happened if the Lionheart had defeated Saladin.

He continued walking. The path was steep but he was in good condition and had no need to hurry. After all, no one was expecting him. He took each step carefully, treading each foot firmly on the ground, making sure he was stable before transferring his weight forward onto the next foot.

The wall seemed easily surmountable, he thought. He went into the forest at the town's edge and it did not take long to find a big enough branch that he could carry back to the château. Propping the log against the wall, Cameron tried climbing up it but the log just kept shifting around, throwing him from one side to another. This was not going to be easy.

Cameron found the unlocked door a few minutes later and was surprised that it could be opened. Hadn't he checked this a few moments ago? His blood was pumping hard in his veins and it was obvious his adrenalin levels must be sky high. In this state he was not so confident of his memory.

Shutting the door carefully behind him, Cameron stayed crouched down at the edge of the wall, expecting guard dogs to come running up to him. After what seemed like half an hour he moved left, keeping close to the wall, feeling an attraction towards the side of the château, away from the main gate. He decided to cross towards the building by some trees. As he left the security of the wall and headed in, his feet seemed to stop just next to a large tree. He wanted to move forward but his feet felt as if they were stuck on the ground. Well, if he could not move forward, the only safe thing to do would be to duck down out of site, so he sat down cross-legged on the grass.

His inner intuition had caused him to stop here. Remaining still, there must be something odd here. He listened carefully but nothing drew his focus. He looked around at the moonlight scene. He was sitting amongst the trees, which were close to the perimeter wall. Just beyond was an open grass space about fifteen meters across, and the château beyond that. His attention was caught by the bark of a pine tree just next to him. Looking up at the dark bark, at regular intervals, small patches of light, no bigger than a fingernail, were shining in the moonlight. They were about fifteen centimeters apart going in a vertical line up the side of the tree to a height of about one and a half meters. It was clear from the regularity of the markings that only a machine could have done this. But what was it for?

Taking a small twig off the ground, Cameron poked the end of the branch at the nearest shiny spot on the bark. As he moved the twig around, he heard a hissing sound of fast moving air, then a small dart the size of a small finger landed in the bark of the tree where the shiny spot was. Cameron stayed still, waiting for any sort of a reaction. He looked at the dart and used his twig again waiving it around the spot where the dart was. The same hissing sound occurred and another dart pounded on the tree trunk next to the previous one.

So the marks on the tree were evidence of a nasty defense mechanism that shot multiple darts. Could he jump through, relying on speed to carry him past the darts? He did not want to try it. He needed some sort of a shield.

This was not going to be too difficult. He went back to the door in the wall, propping it open with a stone. Looking around he went outside again and retrieved the branch he had used to try and scale the wall. He shut the door behind him and took the branch across to the tree. He held the branch vertically, stood it in line with the markings on the tree and then slipped between the branch and the tree trunk. He heard several darts thudding into the branch, but none touched him.

He placed the branch on the ground and walked across the grass. As he drew close the grandiose building rose before him. The gloom suited the castle, giving it an impression of a malevolent power. He did not like the building.

He looked straight ahead and examined the rocks at the bottom of the château. The stone was craggy, leaving some parts jutting out several meters away from the château walls above. In between the rocks were dark spaces where he could see nothing.

As he turned round the corner of the château, his instinct told him to approach the subsequent next dark space. He moved forward step by step into the darkness and stopped for a moment to give his eyes a chance to adjust. He could hear an owl hooting in the distance despite the distraction of the thumping of his heart.

He felt his way forward, his eyes finding the shape of a door at the base of the rocks. When he was right up to the door he stretched his hand out and touched it. It was an old heavy wooden door with iron fittings. He turned the handle. The door opened with a small creaking noise.

Cameron walked forward and stretched out his hand to touch the doorframe. The outside of the frame was wooden as well but the inside of the frame was metal with small holes in it. He realized these would be where motion detectors were located and as soon as he stepped through the door, they would be set off. Then again, wouldn't there have been cameras and motion detectors all around the castle to locate intruders long before he got this far? Hadn't he set off the motion detectors by opening the door and moving his hand across the holes? He stepped over the threshold, stood still and waited. Nothing happened. The silence continued.

He did not switch his torch on, wanting to keep his night-sight for as long as possible. He sensed rather than saw a long thin corridor stretching out ahead, and started to make his way along it.

At first, he felt as if the air was rushing along the corridor and out of the building. As he concentrated he realized that it was energy and not air, and it was rushing at him. As he paid attention, he started seeing pictures moving toward him, pictures of headless devils with knives.

Picture after picture came his way, each more bloody and horrifying than the last. But they awakened no fear in him, he just kept moving forward, sliding his feet along the smooth floor. He focused his attention on his feet and the feeling of this floor, making sure he did not fall down steps or run flat into a dead end.

He then began expanding out his heart energy, pushing out so as to form a bubble of white light in front of him. This energy grew, until it was as wide as the corridor in which he was walking. The horrific picture show coming at him seemed to melt as soon as it came anywhere near this white energy.

As he moved forward, there came a point when he could no longer feel the walls on either side of him. The air was different and he realized he was moving into an open chamber. The horror pictures seemed to disappear at this point. Now he sensed a different problem: he could hear something growling in the darkness. He checked his senses to see whether this was a real growl or just a noise in his imagination. It was real.

Standing at the doorway of a room in the dark with a growling animal in it was stupid, so he had to risk losing his night-vision. Being careful to close his eyes first, he switched on his torch. He opened his eyes to slits to find a small chamber carved out of the solid rock, with smooth stone walls on all sides, two doors going off the wall opposite him and a black Labrador in the middle of the room snarling at him.

Keeping his eye on the dog, he felt around in the pocket of his coat for some kind of weapon. Keys in the left pocket were useless. In his right pocket he felt a package that he did not recognize and took it out. There, melting into its wrapping paper was the smelly Munster cheese sandwich he had been given by the boy on the tractor. He noticed that the dog stopped growling when he brought out the sandwich. He placed it on the ground just one pace in front of him. The dog walked cautiously up to the cheese, picked up the sandwich in his mouth and started chomping on it. Cameron stood fascinated. His heart opened and he beamed his energy at the dog. He had never thought that an animal with such a sensitive sense of smell would eat Munster cheese. Perhaps this 'guard dog' was just very hungry and would eat anything. He almost started giggling at the absurdity of it.

The dog finished eating, turned tail and ran out of the door on the left, not paying him any more attention. The door through which the dog went had an open ironwork grill so Cameron went up to it and closed it. It was unusual to have a Labrador as a guard dog, but he would prefer that he could do a little exploring around here without having to worry about the dog coming back.

Cameron turned towards the other door. It looked like it was made of solid wood, probably oak, with metal hinges. The handle turned easily, being well oiled, and he went in.

He shone his torch around to see what awaited him. The room was a small amphitheatre, semi-circular in shape with about forty upholstered chairs. At the front was a small table covered in a red velvet cloth. On it there was a piece of crystal. The atmosphere in the room was thick, highly charged, as if electricity was being generated in a room next door.

Taking his first steps into the room, he felt as if he had walked into a thick black fog, so dense and heavy was the character of the chamber. He tried to remember what it was like just outside the room. Emptiness. It was as if nothing could penetrate in here.

He went up to the crystal. It was carved in the shape of a skull, just like in his dream. It was real! After this long trip, he had a sense of satisfaction on seeing that the skull existed. As he picked the heavy quartz up, the skull seemed to vibrate in his hands. It made the whole of his body vibrate, even enlivening his feet. This was worth the journey! The crystal seemed to be the only thing that could resist the oppressive darkness in the room. He could feel the skull trying to speak to him. He did not hear a voice but as he opened up his mind he could feel a clear message saying go quickly, danger ahead.

Cameron put the skull in his rucksack and slung it over one shoulder. All his back felt as if it were on fire from the closeness of the object. He turned towards the door and at that moment the lights came on.

A man stood in the doorway, a shock of straight black hair on his head. He was small and thin, slightly lop-sided in the way he was standing, with a cane in one hand and a pistol in the other.

"Dans le temps, on avait coupé les mains des voleurs! Mais – putain, qui êtes – vous?" he spat out.

"Your history is bad, they only used to cut off one hand, not two," said Cameron. At the same time, he brought his rucksack around to his front and in one smooth movement, he slid the crystal skull into his hands, letting the rucksack dangle from one arm. He held it in front of him carefully, so the skull was always between him and the man with the gun. The man moved his arm to point the gun at Cameron's head, but Cameron just moved the skull up. He was sure the man would not shoot if there was a risk of damaging the skull. It was irreplaceable.

"I order you to put that down." Cameron had never heard such authority in a voice and for a single instant, he hesitated. Then he let the power of it wash over him and smiled to himself.

The smile seemed to drive the man to a bursting anger. He was used to being obeyed. His face went all red and he almost shouted his words, struggling for control. "I am going to enjoy feeding your giblets to the pigeons. Hesitate, what do you think you are going to do, just ease out of here with my possessions, motionless? I wonder, you could walk round and round the gardens, such pretty plants, have you ever seen the roses, each petal perfect in its stationary splendor, stay and watch the colors enfold, you will not get very far!"

Cameron felt his head go fuzzy. He realized the man was trying to hypnotize him. He shook his head violently to clear it, not that there was much effect to clear. The man was either incompetent at it or was not efficient on the spur of the moment. The man noticed the change and his tone went hard "If the dogs don't get you, the police will. Now put it down."

For once in his life, Cameron was at a loss for words. It was against his morals to "steal' something and he just wanted to get out of the room. There was no point in arguing with this man, every second of delay increased the likelihood of the security guards turning up. He needed to go fast. "You should have kept the skull up in your office. What was it down here for, some sort of black magic ritual in this chamber of darkness? Your Labrador was hungry."

Cameron did not wait for him to digest this but ran at the man, holding the skull in front of him. As he placed his left foot forward, a voice, sounding through time and space echoed one word into the chamber, "Jump". With athletic limbs from weeks of cycling, he launched himself up, pedaling his legs to gain height. At the same time he heard a loud explosion and realized the man had fired the gun. He traveled far enough to crash into the figure, bringing them both to the floor. Cameron was first to his feet. He saw the gun lying to one side and kicked it out of the way into the gloom under the chairs. The man was groping on the floor, winded from the collision.

Cameron slid the skull back into his rucksack, and turned round to speak to the prone figure. "Your time is over. Take better care of your dog."

He strode out of the room, trying to appear calm but once out of sight he was desperate to get along the passageway as quickly as possible. Once outside he looked across trying to find the branch he had dropped next to the tree. He felt the skull leaving impressions in his head again. Following its indications he ran down the main drive. As he got to the gate he turned and ran along the inside of the wall, going back out to the street via the same doorway he had user to enter. He started to run down the road into town but after fifty meters he turned and ran back the same way, following the instructions from the skull. He ran up the road and then took a flying leap into the forest, traveling as fast as he could. He thought he heard the sounds of animals rustling behind him. The skull gave him a clear picture of tracker dogs catching his scent, running backwards and forwards along the road and then getting confused in the forest, too many other smells obscuring his trail.

Cameron strode forward through the moonlight trees in the cool air of the night. The forest beckoned.

21

Elaine's Reception

Elaine woke up with a crick in her neck, annoyed that she had fallen asleep when so much excitement was going on. She sat back and watched what was happening around her. They were all busy, three or four to a terminal, discussions flowing backwards and forwards, vigorous pointing at the screens, occasional high fives to celebrate an achievement. Only Mole was not in sight.

Malika appeared and beckoned Elaine over. Elaine left the room and they walked down the corridor.

"Your grandfather wants you to join him. He is currently in a hologram remote session with his group. When you go in there, be careful. It is possible but unlikely that the hologram can be traced, so they are all being extra careful about what they say. You should be able to follow it though. I'll help if you need any special translation." Malika grinned at her.

They went through a non-descript door into a small room. There sat Mole on a simple basket chair next to a round glass table. Above its surface shone the hologram video. She could see imagines of eleven figures, all sitting down on basket chairs similar to Mole's. The hologram video had been set up to show the figures about thirty centimeters tall. They were all green, which surprised Elaine. She had expected a full spectrum high definition Hologram Video with these high tech types. The video timing was high speed, and the figures moved without any sign of jerkiness.

Mole broke off the current conversation and brought Elaine forward. "Come in my dear. Friends, this is my granddaughter Elaine. It is she who unlocked the door to the coffins."

At once all the figures stood up. Elaine raised her eyebrows in surprise.

A petite Asian woman started speaking. "Elaine, my name is Suki. We asked your grandfather to bring you here. I cannot name all the people in this H.V., but around this virtual table are some legends in the Net world. We have been trying for years to break into the Golden Coffins, as we call them, and you have succeeded where we all failed. We want to thank you from our hearts and tell you what we have done with your gift.

"Every piece of information in the Coffins is being dumped out into friendly Clouds. From there it is being rapidly duplicated. It was slow work at first as they had limited external access points and we did not want to overload them in case they noticed the slow performance and realized someone was in their systems. Then one of our Russian friends noticed that they had satellite interfaces installed but were not using them. So we pumped everything out that way.

"We are getting a mountain of information about one of the most malicious groups in the world. We think that evidence of all their activities will be revealed. As soon as the hackers have brought some stability to the databases, we will have political experts, human rights fighters and lawyers starting analyzing everything. In a few hours over a thousand trusted free people will be engaged with this data."

"But what about Ca…" Mole glared at her before she could complete Cameron's name.

"Mole has kept us informed about your personal concern in this matter. He has been and gone from the place you expected him. They have already contacted the police and an international arrest warrant is being prepared on the charge of burglary. The warrant will be challenged in the courts in France and England. He is accused of stealing a valuable object from the château. But they seem to have been too hasty. The fact that there is no recorded electronic evidence is going to make this charge rather easy to dispute. We will have a counter strategy in action within forty-eight hours. For now, we hope he can remain hidden."

"He's my friend. Please look after him."

"We will," replied Suki.

Elaine stood up "I'll let you get on with your planning then." As she got up and walked towards the door, her thoughts were with Cameron, wondering what was happening with him.

22

At the Castle Gardens

Cameron woke up and looked around him, not sure for a moment where he was. The room was warm and he was comfortable in bed under a large duvet. The walls around were all white with a few tasteful oil paintings of forest scenery. He stood up and went to look out of the window. A tram clattered by, its destination marked on the front, Heidelberg. Now Cameron remembered: he was in Handschuhsheim, a small town just next to Heidelberg in Germany. He was in the hotel where he had worked as a student. He was safe and had slept at last.

Cameron had spent almost thirty-six hours getting here. After leaving the château he had walked straight up a path that led away from the town and into the forest. He had crossed over a hill and followed a footpath down into the next town. Moving through the forest at night was nerve-wracking after his confrontation in the château; there were so many noises around. He enjoyed Nature but this was a foreign place with unexpected sounds, plus he was mentally exhausted and concerned that someone was following him. He suspected a wild boar had moved past him in the night, detecting a grunting sound only a few meters away. He arrived in the small town the other side of the mountain still under the cover of night, and went through the empty main street until he found the bus stop. He checked the timetable and went back in to the forest for cover. He waited, sat with his back against a tree until five minutes before the bus was due to arrive. He walked down to the town and got on the bus without incident.

After that, always moving in small amounts, a bus here, a train there, he continued his journey. He crossed into Germany on foot across an unmarked green border, anonymously, no passport control being present. He did not know if someone was trying to follow him but if they were, he would make it as difficult as possible to detect his whereabouts.

He remembered Heidelberg as magical, so that was where he headed. He was tired and needed somewhere safe to sleep, so he journeyed just north of the town to Handschuhsheim, which was quieter than the touristy Heidelberg. He was still remembered at the hotel from his student days, so when he checked in he did not have to show his passport. No-one could trace him to this building, so he could rest in peace.

His difficulty now was that he just did not know what to do with the skull. He had traveled all this way, and confronted so many barriers, both in his own mind and in the outside world. He had taken so much time getting to the point where he had the crystal skull that he had not spent any effort on working out what to do with it when he got it.

There it was lying on the floor still in the rucksack. He bent down and took it out. As the skull was exposed to the light of day, it felt as if the whole room became brighter. He looked at the skull and felt as if his whole being also began to glow. He realized this "thing" had real power, a force which gave the owner a huge advantage over others. The owner could manipulate individuals and force them to do their will.

For a second he was tempted to keep it for himself. He laughed the temptation away. He had given up too much to stray now from his chosen path and turn into a dictator. The moment passed.

He formulated a question in his mind. Once he felt the force of the question was strong enough, he opened up his mind to the skull and let it hang in the air: what do I do with a crystal skull?

He felt pictures coming into his mind. Pictures of the castle in Heidelberg. The pictures did not just come to his mind but seemed to appear in his heart first. Along with the pictures he knew things: he was to go to the castle gardens with the skull.

Cameron put the skull back in the rucksack, got dressed and went outside. Just a short distance away was the Tiefburg, a small old castle ruin in Handschuhsheim. He bought some food for brunch at the market in the castle keep and started walking south down the little narrow back roads. Soon the roads faded to a small pathway, which disappeared into the forest. He continued along the forest path, enjoying the sun shining through the trees. The deeper forest was ever-green, but here the wood was mixed growth, giving it a much lighter feel than the dark forests of Hansel and Gretel tales.

Cameron arrived at Philosphersweg, a pathway set on the hillside above Heidelberg. From here the castle on the other side of the valley played peek-a-boo through the trees and houses. After a while, he cut off from the path, descending straight down the hill, until he reached a little path running along the old riverbank.

At the riverside the noises of the town disappeared. Just the peaceful sounds of nature could be heard. The river was much smaller now than when the original banks had been built, leaving room for marsh reeds to grow in the silted up edges and for a large variety of birds to add their cacophony to the day. On the other side of the valley could be seen the beautiful old university town buildings. Standing here in Nature looking across at the ancient buildings, he felt he was almost back in medieval times.

He crossed the river at the old bridge, walked through the cobbled streets full of tourists and took the path straight up to the castle. It was a steep climb. He wandered around the castle buildings but found nothing there that interested him. Then he went into the castle gardens.

The gardens had been constructed some four hundred years previously when the Heidelberg Prince of the Palatinate, Frederick V, had married Elizabeth Stuart, daughter of James 1st of England. There had been an attempt at that time in Heidelberg by the Rosicrucians to bring spiritual-based ideas into the world to influence European culture and politics. The gardens were one example of that movement, each layout of the beds, statues and lawns being highly symbolic. After the completion of the gardens, the castle was at the peak of its splendor. Shortly after, all of it was destroyed in war, and the spiritual movement that it represented died with it. Cameron knew, war was the second best way to destroy good in the world. After fear.

The gardens had been newly rebuilt though, splendid lawns and plants, the biggest attraction for the tourists being a reformed labyrinth. Only the higher parts of the gardens were not renewed, money running out before the project was complete.

He walked over to the wall at the edge of the garden and looked east down the valley. The old town lay just beneath the castle and stretched along the riverside into the mist-covered distance. The Neckar meandered through the reeds in the old river bed. Although it had none of its former might, the river looked splendid surrounded by so much green, making the city even more beautiful. He absorbed this wonderful sight before turning round and wandering back through the gardens.

Here he found peace. It was as simple as that. After all his exertions in recent times, this was a moment where he felt content. He sat and blossomed in the enjoyment of the moment. He shut his eyes and lost himself to time and place.

When he opened his eyes again, the light had changed. There seemed to be no one about. Had he fallen asleep? He wasn't sure. He was just drifting in the lightness of being here. There was an ancient legend that before the castle was built a famous seer had lived here. After feeling the strange lightness around him, he could well believe it.

A rather corpulent woman shuffled past where he was sitting. She was dressed in the simple garb of a traditional Central American Indian. Surprised to see such a costume in this place, he continued staring at her receding back. She stopped walking, turned half-round and looked at him. She did not smile or beckon him, but stared into his eyes before walking away.

His heart seemed to open up. He got up and walked in her direction, keeping his distance.

She walked up to the side of the gardens next to the road towards where the older ruins were. There was a series of broken pillars in a row. The woman headed past the pillars and when she reached the back wall, she stopped next to a man leaning there.

As Cameron walked towards the two of them, he noticed that several others were descending down the stairs leading from either side and from the path on his right-hand side, which led to the castle. The gardens had gone from appearing deserted, to giving off a crowded feeling. About thirty people were standing around with Central American Indians being in the majority.

When he was about five meters away from them he saw that some of the group had formed themselves into two-thirds of a circle, leaving a gap exactly where he was approaching. This circle was a mix of people from all over the world. A few were in western dress. The rest of the group were looking on in silence, standing back from the circle.

As he moved forward towards them, those in the circle all took out small packages that they were carrying, wrapped in what looked like dark silk cloth. Only the woman whom he had seen first did not carry anything but held her arms at her side.

They each unwrapped an object and held it in their hands, each facing into the circle. They were all holding a crystal skull, with the face directed into the centre of the circle. As the skulls came into the fading light, they seemed to glow and together gave off a feeling of energy that made an almost audible hum.

They had come to meet him.

He stopped just short of the incomplete circle. How did they know he would be here? He had not even realized himself where he was going until less than twenty-four hours ago. They must have traveled across the World, keeping their movements secret and the skulls secure. This would have taken months of planning …

Cameron realized the skulls would have told them everything they needed to know. The skulls knew his whereabouts and where he was likely to be. They had had all the information they needed to get here. Also, they must have already known he would be successful in retrieving the skull.

He looked at each skull and the person carrying it. Every skull was unique, with a different color of stone, opaqueness and size. The largest was of full adult proportions, the smallest the same as the skull of a seven year old child. Each person remained passive with no expression of emotion on their faces, not looking at Cameron but into the centre of the circle. The atmosphere was one of calm patience.

Sliding his rucksack off his back, Cameron carefully took out the skull and held it in his hands. His heart glowed, encouraging him. He raised the skull to head height so it was facing him, skull to skull. Inwardly he thanked the skull although at this moment was not sure why. Across the other side of the circle was the woman he had first seen, still holding her arms by her side.

Cameron walked forward and entered the circle. As he progressed he realized that the others were shifting around, completing the circle behind him. As he walked to the woman, her face remained impassive, only her eyes told her tale. She was crying, tears trickling onto her cheeks. Her eyes were full of a mixture of emotions, of unspoken thanks and brimming with happiness. He looked deep into her eyes and saw in the depths all the years of waiting, of hope, pain, joy, doubt, despair, all the expectancy building up for this one moment.

He held his arms straight out in front of him and offered her the crystal skull. Only then did she move her arms up and accept it from him.

After taking the skull she turned it round so it was also facing into the circle. At the same time the circle started to chant in a low gentle way. He did not understand what they were saying. They started singing in different rhythms to each other, in an old polyphonic style. He felt that with all the skulls in place, the circle was complete and somehow their gentle chant harmonized and resonated with that sensation of completeness.

Cameron felt the energy in the circle start to build up. He looked at the woman in front of him and put his hands together in the Asian symbol of greeting and bowed to her. He turned around intending to walk out of the circle back the way he had come. In the centre of the circle a beam of light was forming. It was about two meters high and sixty centimeters in diameter.

Cameron was not sure what to do and turned to look at the woman. She looked him in the eyes and nodded once towards the beam of light. He understood. After a small hesitation, he stepped into the beam.

From outside it looked as if the beam was coming out of the ground and going up into the heavens. Inside, he realized that there were two beams and that the stronger one was coming down from above into the ground. He sensed this beam passing through the whole of his head. It emptied his head of all the weak junk thoughts that were there, burning them away. The light was fierce and came down to his chest. It was as if his body was being cooked in a celestial microwave. He began to laugh at the thought, giggling as he stood there. The light continued moving down, going through his abdomen. It seemed as if all the ill-feelings, the resentments and anger he had built up in his life were all being burnt away. This was harder to cope with and he had to adjust to a scary awareness of release, as if he was letting go of his very being. His laughter changed its tone, going from a nervous chortle into a last madcap laugh.

He gave in. Awash in this strange light, standing in this circle of strangers, by the broken pillars of a half-restored garden, far from any place he would call home, he let go of every feeling and thought he had ever had. He sensed everything leaving as the sheer power of this light bathed him in its celestial purification, washing him clean.

His head became very pleasantly empty, the usual everyday thoughts removed and only a vast consciousness remaining.

As the light penetrated down and washed through his legs, he felt himself give a final let go. He looked up and cried out, his last pain and agony released in one long howl. Exhausted, he sank to his knees and then down onto the ground.

At the Castle Gardens

23

Awakening

When Cameron woke up, it was dark and the gardens were deserted. He sat up slowly but even this gentle movement caused his head to spin. He felt detached from himself. It wasn't that his head was dizzy. In fact his head felt empty, an emptiness that was full, or perhaps a fullness that was empty. How wonderful! His feeling of dizziness increased as his mind wandered around and he realized he needed a new area from where to fix his viewpoint. His consciousness wandered until it reached his heart. There he found a ball of golden fire, fixed in the space where his heart was. Focusing on this held him in place.

The skull was gone. He would not see it again. Well, he might. He was connected to the skull now, and he thought that if he ever needed to see it again, a way would be open to do so. For now, it was in the right hands, and he was content with that.

He got up, being careful not to make any sudden movements with his head, which would set off his dizziness again.

He knew the castle gate would now be locked. While wondering how to get out, he felt a picture of a pathway in the woods just above the gardens come into his mind. In going through the forest and heading west, he would come out at a road and then could make his way down to the town.

He moved up into the woods and walked forward. There was a certain amount of light from the waning moon, enough to pick his way between the trees. Here was a deciduous forest, with a light blanket of fallen leaves on the floor. He was not afraid of tripping up over anything. It was as if he knew where to place his feet so that he could walk smoothly forward.

He was also aware of the plant and animal life around him. The trees felt alive, brimming over with energy into an almost thinking consciousness. He could not see the animals as such; he just knew where they were. Interestingly, the animals seemed to be unaffected by his presence. A rodent ran across his path, brushing against his shoe. Rather than shying away, the animal life just ignored him, knowing he presented no danger to them.

He came out on to a road, and made his way down into the valley below and into the old town. The first buildings appeared at the side of the road. As he passed by he realized he could sense the energy coming off each building. He could feel the quality of each house, what sort of people were attracted to live there, and a general sense of the history of each construction: whether good or bad things had happened, were the owners contented or angry, loving or self-interested, had a group of people spent years in God-devoted prayer in a house, or had a murder been committed in one.

He arrived at the central pedestrian road, where more people were on the streets. As they walked passed him, he found he could read their minds. He felt their current emotional situation, what they were worried about or what they were concentrating on. As the road became crowded, he found it confusing and overwhelming, like moving into a multi-colored fog. He diverted into a side street and then across the bridge to the quieter part of the city. There he took the riverside path Southwest.

What to do next? He was not overly concerned. There seemed to be nothing to worry about. The most pressing thing to do would be to find a place to sleep. A small hotel nearby would do. There was no reason to go back to the hotel in Handschuhsheim. Then it was time to go back to England. But how, with the authorities probably looking for him? It would not be possible to fly or take the boat over the channel. The chances of being stopped would be too high. He needed someone who had no problem helping a fugitive from the authorities. In his mind a picture of a building appeared. With the picture of the building came the knowledge of who was inside and how he would gain entrance. He smiled, both on his face and in his heart, a deep contentment that the answer to such a difficult problem had been given to him. Even if the answer was completely mad.

24

Shark's Place

Shark read his latest messages from the Com and turned to look out of the window at the rooftops over Hamburg. Up here at the top of the building the walls had a fresh coat of paint, with a bizarre mixture of bright colors randomly splattered over the walls. The decorators must have had fun, as most of the original black floor was awash with the same assortment of pigments, this time looking as if someone had been spreading heaps of paint on the ground and then sliding around on their backsides in the mess. At first glance, the only thing that stood out from the colors was the latest, top-of-the-range Com equipment on the simple wooden tables. Anyone taking a closer look, however, might have spotted the small wires taped to the corners of the windowpanes. This place was wired like a spy centre, but geared to keep other spies out.

Shark contemplated what he had just read. Mole and the Knights had made a major breakthrough. There were three excited lawyers working next-door pawing over various documents that the Knights had passed on to them. The rest of the lawyers were working from home. The hackers were probably asleep; it was the wrong time of the day for them. Shark did not yet foresee the full consequences, but he knew a major change was in motion and he would find out soon enough. Mole was back to high activity and success was a guarantee! Now Mole had sent another request for Shark to consider.

A loud bang at the door preceded its abrupt opening. A tall punk entered the room. His hair was done in a rainbow Mohican with red at the back, through to purple at the front. He wore a torn white t-shirt and drain-pipe trousers above a long pair of pointed shoes.

"Gruss dich Shark!" said Bob.

"I thought you wanted to practice your English?"

"You gotta look at this. There's a guy downstairs wanting to speak to the boss."

"So?"

"This guy is dressed like you ain't never seen. Cylinder, coat, calm type, he cool for an over-dressed penguin. He's also speaking bad German in an English accent."

Shark went across to his Com and switched to the view of the security scanners downstairs. Sure enough, there was a strange guy wearing an old-fashioned top hat and tails sitting calmly, while three young punk women stood next to him and not so gently ribbed him. The guy was not bothered by the banter at his expense; he even seemed mildly amused at the humor. He looked somehow familiar. On a hunch Shark asked that he be brought up.

Shark sat down in front of his Com and continued working on it until the man was brought in and invited to sit down by Bob. "Thank you," he said.

"Nothing for no good," replied Bob.

Shark looked at the man to watch his reaction to Bob's English. In front of him was a man dressed in a grey morning-suit with a blue cravat. His face seemed both tired and refreshed. His eyes were odd, with a strange faraway gaze as if he was looking at this room but seeing an old comedy movie playing at the same time. It was obviously a funny film as well.

"You must forgive Bob his English," said Shark, "He learnt it as a child from a rough English lodger his mother used to take in. To improve his speech he did a course on English idioms but decided he didn't like them, so he uses the German ones instead. Direct translation from German is not helpful for foreigners, but we tend to like it."

"What a wonderful cultural mix," said the penguin to Bob.

"I understand only railway station," said Bob. "My English is under all pig. To me it is sausages."

"Sausages?"

A puzzled look appeared on the stranger's face. Shark decided to move things on and asked him what he wanted.

"I have been on a long trip through France next to the Swiss border. I successfully completed a strange task there. However, I probably upset some very powerful people who have the capacity to have the police searching for me in many countries. Therefore I need to get back to England without using my official ID. I need either a fake ID or a safe passage across the channel. Can you help me at all?"

"What's your real name and what makes you think we can help?" asked Shark.

"My name is Cameron Trevelyn." He paused. "I don't know if you can help me. I was in Heidelberg wondering how to get back to the U.K. when in my mind's eye I saw a picture of a building with two eyes and ears that had smoke coming out of them and a peculiar electronic scream coming from it. When I asked people in Heidelberg whether they had heard of such a building, they all knew this place. It seems to be quite famous. So I took the train up to Hamburg and here I am. I did not see any ears or eyes when I came in though."

Shark worked the Com some more before going on with his questioning, "Do you always dress like that?"

"No," replied Cameron, "I knew I needed some sort of device to gain your attention. You would be suspicious of strangers in case they were working with the police. I figured out this outfit was too obvious for the police to use and at the same time harmless."

"Wait a minute, please," said Shark as he carried on manipulating his Com. He paused, gathering his thoughts about what he had found. Finally he turned round and gave his full attention to Cameron. "This house is used by those who have had enough of today's society and want a break. It's mostly punks and those who have an anarchist's mind-set. Anyone who does not like this or any other government. We've been going for years and many of the older characters live close by. The police attempt to raid us now and again so we have developed a safety mechanism, whereby all the metal shutters in the building come down and the steel doors shut. Someone decided to paint eyes and ears on the outside of the appropriate shutters. A screaming siren goes off which alerts our friends in the area who surround the building to give the police a hard time. Later on someone added a switch to the wood oven so that the smoke gets diverted from the chimney to pipes, which exit at the windows where the ears are painted. We find the whole effect is intimidating. That keeps the number of official visits down and leaves us in peace."

"Quite an impressive organization," answered Cameron.

"Organization? We don't like organizing much, we just do what we want and are prepared to put a bit of energy into being left alone."

"Can you help me?" asked Cameron again.

The room went quiet.

"Do you have any money?" asked Shark.

"Almost none. I had to risk a credit card to buy these clothes," answered Cameron.

Shark worked his Com again, pressed a few commands in and then spoke at the machine, "Anyone observing us?"

"Look to your left. They have been in that car so long we thought they were going rusty," came the voice back through the Com.

The keyboard rattled as Shark banged the keys again before giving out is order, "All lights on orange, we're expecting visitors."

Bob became alert at this, jumping to his terminal and repeating the command in German, a big smile on his face.

He turned to Cameron again. "The police have this building permanently monitored and often note who goes in and out. A friend of ours keeps us informed about who is being pursued, as many of us are frequently on the wanted list and it's good to know when we need to lie low for a while. Your clothes got you noticed by us but they will also get you noticed by the police, who happen to be sitting outside. I checked, they already have your name, so it won't be long before they find out what clothes you bought and then realize from the description that you entered this building. The message I just sent is to the community here. Orange light means we are expecting a police raid any minute and they should prepare for immediate confrontation."

"So runs the rabbit," grinned Bob at Cameron.

Cameron's face dropped, "I don't want anyone to get hurt for my sake. I would prefer to give myself up to the police and take my chances there."

Shark shook his head, keeping an expressionless face. "The community will gather and fight because they want to. Some hate the police so much they cannot wait to have a go at them. Others will do it because they want to defend our lifestyle. The rest simply want a fight. This has nothing to do with you, none of them know you are here. They will be doing it for their own reasons. And if they don't want to fight then no one will be outside at all, though I think that is unlikely. We have not had a battle with the police for several months and some are itching to have a go."

"With us is not good cherry eating," said Bob in agreement.

Cameron looked out the window. Everything seemed quiet. He thought he felt an increase in tension in the atmosphere but it was slight enough that it could just have been his imagination. He looked across at Shark, who was busy talking to several different people. They all arrived at the door, had a short conversation with him and then disappeared again. For a society of anarchists, Shark looked rather like a leader to Cameron.

"This is an odd place to find in a Dome," he said.

Shark frowned. "Most of the people here don't realize they are in a Dome. Just because they cannot stand the society in this city does not mean they are ready for outside life. So here is a sort of way station, a half-way house for them. That's our basic function.

"Bob will take you through an underground tunnel to a safe house nearby. From there you will go to a small fishing village in Ost-Friesland where you will stay for a few days with a woman friendly to us."

"She has a stack of wood in front of the cottage," said Bob.

"Sounds idyllic," replied Cameron.

Shark grinned, noticing Cameron was taking Bob literally. "From there, we can put you on a boat. You will be transferred from vessel to vessel until we can set you on an English boat that can sail back into its own harbor, without being noticed. It's a bit of a long way round, I am afraid, but a direct trip might attract attention. This way we have found to be better."

"I am very grateful, you are exceedingly generous. But you know I have no money - why are you doing this for me?" asked Cameron.

"I found out who you are, your face already looked familiar. One of your students is working with a friend of mine, Mole. He's quite a character; you will already know his public persona. I think you'll be surprised at what he can do. Mole will get someone to pick you up when you arrive in England. Perhaps he will even meet you himself. That he requests your assistance is reason enough to help you. But my feeling is that your task has changed something significant, and the world is a better place for it. So I want to help."

Cameron shook his head, "All I have done is to remove a power from those who would control others. They are weakened but are still influential in the world."

Outside a red light started flashing and the shutters on the windows started rattling as they came down. A screeching siren went off outside, drowning the sound of the approaching police cars.

Bob looked out of the window while he still could, "There we have the lettuce." He went across to the chimney stack and after playing with a metal lever, part of the wall slid open, "It is all about sausages. Highest Railway! Komm, hier runter," he said.

Cameron looked across at Shark. "What did he say? Sausages again? You really want me to go down there?"

"Inside the chimney stack you will find a ladder built into the wall," said Shark. "The smoke from the chimney is already diverted to the outside windows so you will be able to breathe. The chimney goes down into the cellar tunnels. There is your escape route. I am afraid that some of them are sewage pipes but you can clean yourself at the other end. No one is about to follow you."

Cameron understood - the famous smoking building was just a way of using their escape route. He grinned at Shark, nodded his head and then followed Bob into the chimney.

25

Meeting at the Harbor

Cameron got off the boat and stood on the harbor pier. It was a grey November morning, with the wind blowing in from the sea and up towards the nearby hills. A few seagulls decorated the small fishing boats along the pier. Beyond, the harbor town was made up of small stone houses, of a type that seemed to have always existed here in the Cornish coastal towns.

It had been a long journey. He had been taken to the German coast and put in a boat. However, the boat journeys were slow. He was transferred from one vessel to another, sometimes at night in a harbor, sometimes on the open sea. Five times he had to jump from boat to boat. Inside each one, it was always the same. Cramped uncomfortable quarters, the stink of fish, little to do and no contact with the outside world.

He wasn't bothered, though. He had a new sense of inner silence, and the journey had been a good opportunity to get used to it. Although isolated and dependent on strangers, he always felt safe.

Cameron sauntered into town, past a few fishing boats, getting used to being back on firm ground. He still carried his small rucksack on his back, but nothing else. The only addition he had acquired in the days of traveling was a small beard. After being at sea his ears were alert to the noises of civilization, but even with all his new heightened awareness he failed to hear the e-car behind him until it was alongside.

The rear window opened, and a familiar voice from inside gave out a joyous yell, "Are you going to get in or do you want to walk all the way?" He looked down at the window and saw a young face, grinning, the eyes twinkling up at him. The last person he had expected to see was Elaine. He grinned back, delighted, then ran round the car and got into the front seat.

He did not have time to put his seat belt on before the car took off, throwing him into the seat. He had thought that this type of e-car could not accelerate quickly but this one must have been subject to some homemade corrections. First he had been rolling backwards and forwards in boats, then after ten minutes on hard ground, he was being rocked around in a doctored e-car with a pupil in the backseat who should probably still be in school!

Once he had buckled himself in, he turned to look at the driver. An older man, mid-fifties, stocky build, his face recognizable as the former education minister, Alan Howarth.

Cameron paused and regained his composure. He opened up his new awareness to the people in the car.

It came to him that even though they had not met before, Alan had been involved in his journey. As a politician, he was careful about what he said to whom, so it was advisable not to be demanding of him. Elaine, on the other hand, was bursting to say what had happened, even if Alan did not agree. There was a strange connection between the two of them. Ah yes, they were close relatives. Father? No, he had met the father before. Grandfather? Yes, maternal grandfather. Well, even to her fellow students she had never boasted that her grandfather was a politician. That must have needed a great deal of self-discipline for a teenager. This was very interesting.

Cameron looked between the two, smiling, then he spoke, "So, our absent student has a famous ex-cabinet minister for a grandfather. You have done well to keep this fact quiet, Elaine."

Mole passed a quick glance Cameron's way before concentrating on the road again.

Elaine looked curiously at him before replying, "I always talk about my Granddad. But to me, he is my friend. When I was younger I spent as much time as possible with him. He told me lots about his young life as a hacker called Mole, so that's what I always ended up calling him. He gave me a new look on life. I always felt accepted with him." Elaine beamed in Mole's direction. "I wasn't that secretive at school. I was always asking friends to come away for the weekend to meet my friend Mole, but they never seemed to find the time. Pity, I wanted to see their faces when they met a famous politician!"

"Ex-politician. You already knew I was Elaine's grandfather?" asked Mole.

"Let's say, it just came to me," answered Cameron. "I would guess as well that when you were a hacker, you got to know people from all over the world, including Hamburg?"

"Yes, it was from my hacker days that I first met the man you know as Shark," said Mole. "We became very good friends over the years and when my government folded, I went back to my old way of life and put energy into contacting old friends. I asked Shark to watch out for you, and he told us you would be arriving here. When Elaine found out, she wanted to pick you up herself. I am afraid that the police have an international arrest warrant for you, so you cannot just walk back into your old house and job. You are most welcome to stay with us for a few days until the situation has cleared up."

"That's very kind of you."

"For one who helped us get rid of the Golden Dead, it's the least we can do."

"Who are the Golden Dead?" asked Cameron.

"When I was a hacker, a group of us were interested in finding out who decided what. There were so many political decisions being made in the executive levels of governments which were never even put before the public to vote on. These decisions had long-term implications for the societies involved, and it seemed that multiple governments would often approach the same topics in the same way. We decided to explore the Net, looking for connections between people and these decisions. We had the advantage that we were working illegally and had no compulsions about breaking into any Network we wanted. Gradually we realized that there were a few very well-protected Com machines dotted about the world, which we could trace messages to and from. The messages going out went to top influential people who stood behind the political leaders, mostly political advisers and members of high-level think tanks. These Com machines were so well protected, we never managed to break into them, although we spent a great deal of effort trying to do so. We then searched around to see who they belonged to, and found that they were always very rich people who lived in retreat.

It was very hard to find information about them. It was as if they were wealthy but showing no signs of life. So we called them the Golden Dead and the relevant Com machines we called the Golden Coffins.

"By chance, we happened to be looking at the Golden Coffins again when Elaine got your mail. It was easy to put two and two together and realize you were going into the building of one of the Golden Dead. How did you find them?"

Cameron paused before replying, "I didn't, well at least not deliberately. I just followed my nose and cycled across France." Cameron gave them a brief description of his journey.

Elaine and Mole had been listening intently. Now all three of them paused as Mole drove onto the motorway and went into the guided lane, letting the car and the highway take control. Cameron was wide-awake in the silence. Alan relaxed and turned round in his seat. He questioned Cameron about his adventures and what he knew about the crystal skull. "So, what did you do with the skull?"

"I gave it to its rightful owners," replied Cameron. "They seemed to know where to find me and I was quite happy to hand it back to those who could best look after it."

"So you had in your hands one of the most powerful artefacts of a forgotten ancient realm and you just handed it to a stranger?"

"Yes," answered Cameron.

"Did you not ever consider keeping it and using it for yourself? Wouldn't such a tool be of tremendous use, never mind the power you had to wield?" asked Mole.

"This skull never felt like it belonged to me. Therefore it would not have been right to keep it, no matter what it could do, or how powerful it made me. So I gave it to those I considered to be the rightful guardians."

Mole looked out the window, contemplating. From here, all that could be seen were the surrounding wheat fields and a few scattered trees in the distance. "I guess I spent too many years amongst politicians. Most of them would grab at power as soon as it is dangled in front of them. It's been a long time since I've seen anyone take such a moral stance in their deeds."

Elaine could not keep still. "We helped too!" She leaned forward towards the front seats, the words bursting forth. "I showed Mole how to break into the Golden Coffin. We hacked it and shut all their defense systems down for you. We even fed the guard dogs sedatives."

Cameron turned to Mole. "How on earth did you do it?"

Mole chose his words carefully. "We could easily monitor the traffic going to and from the Golden Coffin as we had isolated its physical connections. We were still having a great deal of difficulty with its encryption techniques. Luckily, just after we knew about you, someone logged onto that Golden Coffin, so we had the basis of how their logon handshake worked. The rest Elaine did for us."

"I could see what the codes were," said Elaine. "I knew the numbers were right and when we tried it, we saw it worked. It was pure intuition - it's what I learnt from you. I always knew I was intuitive but what I learned from you was to trust that intuition and not be afraid of it."

Mole continued the story. "Inside a system, there are usually extra layers of protection but these were not being used on the Golden Coffin. We had complete access to the whole of their functionality. I guess they were so arrogant and thought that no one could hack through their defenses, so they did not bother with internal security. Big mistake.

"We spent a few hours looking round their systems before deciding what to do. We just switched off the entire perimeter wall monitoring for the château by making it look like a security maintenance update. We then fed the guard dogs using a sedative program used for when the vets are called in. We upped the dose of the sedatives and then let the dogs loose in the grounds so they would fall asleep outside where they would not be noticed. Without any input from the Coms, the security guards would not be aware of your presence. Finally, we thought you might head for the cellar meeting room so we shut down all the motion detectors around it. That's about it."

"We were great!' added Elaine.

"Yes, you were," agreed Cameron. "Impressive. I couldn't have done it without you. Did you do anything else while in their systems?"

"We did a complete dump of their databases. We could also easily get into the other Golden Coffins and extract their data too. We called in a few other hacker teams around the world who knew about the Golden Coffins, and within six hours we had copies of everything they had ever stored, parked in a pyramid of data dumps throughout the world. So now the hacker community have access to the details of every transaction that the most secretive society has ever made. You can be sure we're going to use it.

"Interestingly enough, we found that in every country where they had a base, we also had a large hacker community we had good ties to and could trust. Strange how things mirror each other isn't it? Naturally each hacker community looked at the data from their own country. My friend Suki in the States found something interesting - the minutes of their meetings. It turned out that they were very worried about that energy machine of yours. They knew that if they didn't stop you then they would lose control of the energy supply and with that, control of society. They had a whole range of tactics they were going to throw at you. The change in the education policy was just the first one. Next was a large sex scandal. All the usual dirty tactics.

"Their idea was, as long as you were trying to defend your schools, you wouldn't have time to promote the energy machine. It's interesting that they identified you as the skull robber. Your face must have already been familiar to them. Your arrest warrant is being challenged, lawyer friends are pointing out that there is no evidence that the crystal skull belongs to the said owner. They'll soon be asking why there's no electronic evidence of you being there despite the building having one of the highest security systems in any private residence in the world. We haven't yet pushed this one as we don't yet want to alert them to the fact that their systems have been compromised.

"So what do you intend to do now?" asked Mole.

"Get some sleep. Return to school, when you think it's safe. I guess I should start campaigning against the new government education policy, but I don't have any energy left for that particular task," said Cameron.

Elaine looked at Mole. Mole glanced back at Elaine.

"You've only been gone a couple of weeks but there have been some remarkable changes around here," said Mole. His voice was steady, in a controlled emotionless fashion. "Someone broke into the government systems and managed to piece together all the different pieces of information the government was keeping about each citizen. This was then sent to each individual in a mail. It seems the government was keeping an awful lot more data about people than they had assumed. Not just summaries of relatives, addresses, tax records, but also a breakdown of average shopping details, usual routes to and from work, security ratings, possible terrorist connections, friends, hobbies, credit ratings and so on. The government summary titled "sexual preferences", based on an analysis of shopping statements caused particular upset. Safe to say the security services are very eager to find out who sent the emails. Unfortunately for them, whoever it was used their own portable equipment to access the government Net from an old port in a disused part of the London underground. They look like being untraceable and electronic surveillance teams are looking rather embarrassed at their ineffectiveness in finding out who did it.

"The public was so angry that the government had no option. They had to resign and call a general election before gross public disorder took place.

"So I don't think you have to worry about the new education policy. The next government might well have different ideas."

Cameron pondered these latest developments. He got a clear read from Mole that he was responsible for bringing the government down but was not going to say it was him. Mole had covered his tracks so well that it was unlikely that he would ever be found out. Cameron turned round and looked at Elaine. Elaine returned his glance and held his eyes for a long time. She looked at him both puzzled and enquiring before she formed her words.

"You have changed. There is something much calmer about you. But you were calm before. You are more... still. Yes, 'still' is the right word. What was it? Are you, I mean, I don't know how to say it..."

Cameron gave her a small smile. "You're right, something has happened to me. When I handed the skull over, they performed a small ceremony, with all of the crystal skulls around me, in a circle. Ever since then it has been as if the force in my heart has been opened up a thousand fold. I'm very aware of everything around me. Open to things, so to say. And my head feels empty. Very pleasantly empty, full of a nice nothingness, a real rest from the permanent cacophony of thoughts that were previously there." He grinned.

"Back at school the teachers were always saying you should work and develop your consciousness," said Elaine. "It seems to me you've just been given an extra boost by a collection of ancient stones! This isn't the way we were taught to do things."

"You're right," sighed Cameron. "I'm not happy about the way it went. I didn't want to end up sitting in the middle of some ancient magic ceremony. One of the reasons why I was attracted to the Heart Voyance Schools was that you were very much left to develop your own skills. This was something quite different."

"Perhaps it was just that you had already developed your capabilities," said Alan. "When we got in touch with the school, Melody told us how you were afraid of cycling - yet you followed your intuition and traveled on your bike, facing your fear. It's by overcoming our fears that we develop ourselves as humans. The ceremony with the skulls was just the final push that caused you to be aware of what you had already developed in yourself."

There was a stillness in the car as they all thought about that.

"So what happens? I mean what happens to you next? Where does it go from here?" Elaine asked.

Cameron looked out the window at the beginning of the rain. "I really don't know. Life is like a long journey. Sometimes things go quickly, like cycling down a hill. And sometimes things go badly, like having a puncture in the rain. You never know what tomorrow will bring. You can only try to remain awake for the next moment."

"Why the next moment?" asked Elaine.

"Because that's the point where the story of your life moves on to the next scene."

"Well, I don't want to move on," said Elaine. "It's too exciting around Mole."

"You have a school to go back to. You've had a small taste of what you can do with your increased intuitive abilities. Can you imagine what more you'll be able to do when you develop them further? There are many more people like you out there, real intuitive individuals like yourself. You've not yet used the opportunity to meet them but they're waiting for you - they know from their intuition that you are someone who is worth getting to know. You just need to approach them and you'll find out."

At this Elaine went very quiet and started looking out the window. She remembered enjoying the company of Malika, Jason and Plume, and realized she had spoken too soon, not meaning what she had said. The expression on her face softened as she contemplated going back to school.

26

Mole Mansions

Cameron stayed several days at Mole Mansions, delighted at all the hectic activity around him. The day after his arrival Elaine, and the others from Castleton returned to the school, passing on the news of his arrival back to a rural safe house. Here he was incognito. Most of the people there ignored him, with which he was quite happy. The anonymity was such a strong contrast to his time at school, where he was always a known figurehead.

He wandered between the Machine Room as Mole called it, the large lounge and the kitchen. Long walks through the surrounding countryside brought him special joy. His new ability to appreciate Nature was a gift that he grew to use all the more as time passed. He also liked the fact that, for once in his life, he had nothing to do. Mole's library was astonishingly broad and he found some rare books with which to occupy his time.

He was reading in the library one day when he heard the doorknob turn. Mole came through the door, a newspaper under one arm. "I thought I'd find you here," he said.

"It's rare now to find a whole room dedicated to books. I thought these 'olde worlde' leather high back chairs would be uncomfortable, but now I find they're ideal for reading. And you have such a wide scope of literature, some rare esoteric gems amongst them!"

"I tell everyone who comes here that the ground floor is an open area for them. Very few of them venture out of the Machine Room to this place. It takes an awful lot of dusting to keep everything clean, but I love it. When I took over the building, the library was here, and I left it intact, just switching my own books in.

"I have lots of news for you."

"The warrant's cancelled and I can go home?"

"Not yet. There'll be a court hearing in two days time in Paris, but it is unlikely to be settled then.

"I got a strange message in one of my old mail accounts, which I rarely use. In fact it's probably more than a year since I received a message there. The message was quite simple but cryptic. It requested that the guest be informed that the one united with the twelve are safe in their designated place. That was it. I tried to trace where the message originated from. I got as far as Mexico but then lost track of it. It didn't take much to figure out that you were the guest and you were being sent a message from the region of Central America. Can you do anything with that?"

"I think they are telling me the crystal skulls are now settled back in their established environment."

"The more interesting news for you is in the newspaper." Cameron opened it out and looked at the headline. It was, "New Zealand Government Discovers Free Energy."

"It seems that a teacher from the Heart Voyance School in Auckland was putting in a patent application for your V-Gen machine, when one of the New Zealand government became interested. They contacted the school and things accelerated very fast from there. One of your experts was flown over there and after a few discussions, the government decided to put their full strength behind it. I could imagine Washington wasn't too happy with them, but The Kiwis are so short of fuel that they probably just gave the Americans the dirty finger."

"It still doesn't solve our problem of getting the machine patented elsewhere."

"Oh, as a former politician, I think it gets round that problem nicely. The cat is out of the bag, you have a bona fide patent and a serious backer in the New Zealand government. They cannot be ignored. The Golden Dead loved controlling governments behind the scenes. Playing a game within a game, so to speak. Open conflict is not their cup of tea. It was obvious that they were pretty stuck on how to react to your energy machine. They must have been desperate to attack the schools in such an obvious manner, that's just not their style. Now their power is diminished and with all we know from their databases, we'll soon have them on the run.

"So when people in other countries in the world start hollering for free energy just like they have in New Zealand, it's going to look stupid for any government to say the patent process is blocked. No one is going to stop you now, far from it. The whole bureaucratic process has been unblocked in one go. You have shifted the key log. The seemingly impossible is now possible."

Cameron remembered his chat around the fire in the pub. He wondered if it was Kurt who had flown out to New Zealand?

"Are you not going to rejoin your party and help them form a new government?" asked Cameron.

"No, my time in politics is over," said Mole. "Working full time in a Dome is very strenuous. I'm not sure whether I could do that again. Trying to remain open in the cloudy environment when the people around you are doing little more than trying to stab you in the back. Even the bubble-up process does not protect you fully. I'm not the only one either.

Shark has problems in Hamburg. It is so difficult for a Heart Person to be around such violence as he experiences there.

"You've seen the Axe and the dent in the wall of the Machine Room? One day I came home for the weekend and was just so full of anger that I had to hit the wall with my fist. It was then I knew that I had to quit or risk losing myself in that emotional swamp. I just can't do it."

Cameron looked at Mole. "It's a brave heart person who goes to work full time in a Dome. On my journey I went through many Domes. First countryside, then Dome, then countryside then Dome, and so on. It disturbed me, made me realize what an artificial world we have built. Dome, countryside, it's like black then white. But the Natural world does not have such well-defined borders, or anything so artificial. We're safe away from the cities, and yet, I can't help thinking that we've grown too comfortable. The few attempts we've made at trying to develop the Sleepers have made little impact. We can go in and pick out the stray few like Elaine but the rest are left untouched. Our efforts are not enough."

"And yet, if we could find a safe way of working in a Dome, we could change everything," said Mole. "London has always been the most vulnerable to outside control, and its democratic processes have been kept at rudimentary levels. Most of the Western governments are leaning our way, and if we could get

London reacting positively, we could have a worldwide domino effect. We could have the whole of humanity working from the heart and not the head."

Mole looked at Cameron's face. His eyes were glazed over and he was looking out of the window, but did not see anything out there. He was grinning from ear to ear.

"You've had an idea, haven't you?"

Cameron nodded gently. "Oh yes. It's time for some larger scale intervention. It's time for moving out of our safe havens and taking risks. As you said, a game within a game," he smiled.

27

The Heart of the Dome

Cameron moved from dream world to brilliant sunshine in an instant. His heart was glowing. He could hear the crows outside as they gathered in the nearby trees for their morning chorus. The vivid smells of a musty autumn, fuelled by the overnight rain, poured through the open window. He felt full of joy at being alive.

He knew what today's task was. He sat upright in bed in a cross-legged position. He quickly focused and put out a clear, strong picture of what he intended to do, asking for assistance. He told the Com in Mole's Mansion to plan his route to London. He requested fifteen street plans of London on A4 sheets of paper. The plans should have overlaid on them a red circle, the circle being cantered on Westminster Abbey and represent a radius of five hundred meters from the centre of the circle. The maps were printed out straight away. Dressing, he went downstairs and had a quick breakfast before starting the journey. He wondered who he would meet. For it was clear, this was not a task he could carry out alone.

The train journey passed without incident. Upon arrival in London, he took the underground to Embankment and walked from there. When he reached Westminster Abbey, he joined the small queue of tourists. Business was slow, even for a major church, he thought to himself. Using money was quite common at the Abbey, so it did not appear strange when he used cash to pay to get in. He still did not want to make his presence here known by paying electronically, given that he was still unsure of his legal status.

Stepping into the building, he was struck by the strange atmosphere. His trip through France had made him used to the different moods in churches, from the religious to the touristic qualities, depending on the usage of the building. There was a tension in the Abbey that he could not define. Here was the heart of England, the spiritual centre of the Kingdom. But here also was a fuzziness, as if the country had lost its way and there was no clarity of purpose.

He first walked to the western end of the building. There was a little chapel there used for prayer. Cameron went in and lit a candle. He then headed for the centre of the church, where the Abbey formed a cross. At random he picked a chair and sat down. He shut his eyes and concentrated on centering himself and relaxing. Focusing inwards, he was aware that others were sitting down in the chairs around him. After a while, he heaved a long outward breath like a sigh and realized it was time. He stood up, walked to the front of this section of chairs and looked at those who were gathered there.

There were twelve of them, six men and six women. He looked at their faces and realized he had only met one of them before. One of the strangers stood out and he stared at her. She stared back. She was a tall woman, late forties, solidly built, with large piercing blue eyes. As he looked at her he did not see her, but the vision of a small man, brown eyes, thin and dark hair, dressed in a monk's habit. The picture of the man overlaid the actual woman. It felt as if he had to look through the picture to find the real person behind. The monk and the woman were one and the same. This woman radiated power. He had never felt such energy from a human being before. He gave a short bow of his head and the woman bowed back in acknowledgement, a slight smile on her face.

He turned to the loving face he recognized. She was in her early thirties, with large dark eyes and straight, thick black hair, ending just below her shoulders. Melody beamed when she realized he was watching her. She held her hands in an "X" across her chest, palms inwards, spreading her hands to show her ring-less fingers. Cameron clearly picked up Melody's thoughts, *"It is good to see you again."* He felt the closeness of their relationship, the warmth of love from a fellow human being who has decided they wanted to be with you for a long time.

He turned back to the rest of the group and handed out the maps of London with the red circles on, before addressing them.

"Thank you. Thank you for being here. We want to build an area where good people can work, at this location in the heart of the city and the centre of the government. We have come now to build a Dome within the Dome. But this inner Dome we are to build will be a Dome of pure light. A place for Heart People.

First we will clear out the Abbey. Then we will establish a light source coming down from above and feeding into the Abbey. Then we will create an inner Dome of Light, which will spread out from here, 500 meters in all directions. The Abbey will be the centre of the Dome and will resonate to the surrounding area. The Dome will have a skin, a strict border at its edge."

He divided them up into groups, three people to go into each corner of the abbey. The tall woman he asked to stay where she was and hold the centre.

Cameron would go forward with the group to the altar.

He looked each in the face, an intense eye contact, finishing with the tall woman. "OK, let's go build a Dome."

Appendix

Explanation of the Heart Voyance School.

The idea behind the Heart Voyance School and the descriptions of the thinking taught there are based on the concept of Heart-Thinking, a term used by the nineteenth century Austrian spiritual philosopher Rudolf Steiner. The connection between head-thinking (i.e. normal thinking) and Heart-Thinking was worked out by an American, George O'Neil, and further worked on and published by Florin Lowndes and Mark Riccio.

Using this type of thinking opens up the capacity of having intuitions from the heart. This intuitive ability can grow so much that instead of an Intuition being an instantaneous "Eureka" moment, the Intuition lasts for much longer (minutes) and grows to be a flow of consciousness that streams out from the heart. This flow of consciousness not only provides you with answers to daily issues, it also increases your empathy and ability to live a compassionate life. It is this flow of consciousness from the heart that is called Heart-Thinking.

Bibliography

An Outline for a Renewal of Waldorf Education
Rudolf Steiner's Method of Heart-Thinking and Its
Central Role in the Waldorf School - Mark-
Dominick Riccio, Ed.D. ISBN 1-59196-346-x

A Study Guide for Rudolf Steiner's Heart-Thinking -
by Mark Riccio ISBN 1-59872-505-x

ENLIVENING THE CHAKRA OF THE
HEART The Fundamental Spiritual Exercises of
Rudolf Steiner - Florin Lowndes, Publisher Rudolf
Steiner Press ISBN: 1-85584-053-7.

Web References

The Heart Explosion.

www.theheartexplosion.com

Heart-Thinking.

www.organicthinking.org

The main English website for Heart-Thinking from Mark Riccio.

Heart Work.

www.iitransform.com

For a method of human development that works from the head to the heart, take a look at the International Institute for Transformation.

www.heartmath.org

A website on the intuitive power of the heart.

CPSIA information can be obtained at www.ICGtesting.com
Printed in the USA
BVOW020801270312

286137BV00014B/5/P